'I could show you what it's like to be kissed by a real man, if you've forgotten,' Ross was saying. 'If I made love to you, you wouldn't be undecided about the direction you want your life to take. You'd know.'

It was true. But suddenly the explanation of his behaviour flashed into Zoë's mind, filling her with a sense of disappointment.

'I know what's wrong with you, Ross,' she said shakily. 'I've met men who behaved like this before, but I didn't expect it of you. It's the old tacky story. Your wife's away, and you'll use any pretext to get someone to fill the gap. It's a common enough syndrome, the lonely husband.'

LOVE'S DOUBLE FOOL

BY

ALISON YORK

MILLS & BOON LIMITED
ETON HOUSE   18–24 PARADISE ROAD
RICHMOND   SURREY   TW9 1SR

First published in Great Britain 1991 by Mills & Boon Limited

© Alison York 1991

Australian copyright 1991 Philippine copyright 1991 This edition 1991

ISBN 0 263 77194 6

Set in 10 on 11½ pt Linotron Plantin 01-9108-58571 Typeset in Great Britain by Centracet, Cambridge Made and printed in Great Britain

TO ARDIFUIR
WITH THANKS

PROLOGUE

WHEN Ross first kissed her they were up on the rough, heather-coated hill behind Morag's cottage. They were talking. With Ross it had always been easy to talk. Then his fingers had tightened on her shoulder where his arm so comfortably lay, and he said, looking over Kilbrannon sound at Kintyre silhouetted against the sunset, 'Will you look at that, Zoë? Someone's putting on a special show for us.'

It was as she looked at the sky with its dreamy swathes of gold and aquamarine and glowing rose—really looked at it, felt it, absorbed it—that Zoë realised suddenly that she was happy: she who had come to Arran feeling that she would never be happy again.

She turned to Ross, her eighteen-year-old face aglow from within and not just from the reflected colours of the sky. And it was then that she saw his expression change to a sudden new awareness of her, so that they looked at each other long and deeply until he murmured her name and gently, so gently, leaned forward and kissed her. Perhaps that gentle kiss was all he meant to happen. But in the meeting of their lips friendship ended and something far stronger was born. Startled by the feelings coursing through them, they looked wonderingly at each other again, then wordlessly Ross took her in his arms and Zoë, as she let herself melt into his kiss, felt with every fibre of her being that this was what she had been created for. Love blossomed in her with all the sudden, fragile, incredible beauty of an exotic flower.

Breathlessly Ross broke away to murmur against her

hair, 'I shouldn't be doing this!' But his arms were denying his words as he held her tight against his chest, and she could hear—almost feel—his heart thudding as hers was.

'Don't say that!' she said fiercely.

'I'm not meaning that I regret it. How could I? But you're so young. . .'

She laughed up into his serious grey eyes and ran a teasing hand through the crispness of his russet hair. 'My age is something that will cure itself. Nothing could be more certain. And as for you—twenty-eight isn't exactly over the hill.'

'It's old enough to know that an eighteen-year-old should be handled with care.'

'I don't feel eighteen. After what's happened this summer I feel as old as. . .' She looked around for something to compare herself with, then ran her fingers over the stone on which they were sitting. It was an outcrop of the natural rock formation, breaking through the heather, and its shining smoothness showed that it must have been a convenient away-from-it-all seat for generations of lovers. 'As old as this,' she concluded.

Mention of the summer's happenings had brought the old shadow back to her brow for a moment, and Ross tried to smooth it away with gentle fingers as he said, 'That, too, is what I'm really talking about. You've had your feelings pounded enough this summer since your father died, Zoë. I shouldn't be adding to the turmoil.'

Her young intensity challenged him. 'Ross—you don't know how wrong you are. Have you ever lost anyone you loved? Someone close to you?'

He thought briefly. 'Grandparents, but I was too young to take in what was going on—so no, I don't suppose I have.'

'Then let me tell you just what happens. Your world,

which you took for granted would always be there, is
suddenly shattered. Gone from under your feet. The
person who loved you and whom you loved has been
taken from you—way beyond time and space and touch.
And that's devastating enough. But much more than that
one person has suddenly gone. It's as though all your
capacity to feel anything has gone too. Ross—when I
came up to stay on Arran with Morag, I was like a ghost.
No substance, no thoughts, no emotions—nothing.'

'I know.' Ross looked tenderly at her. 'When I first
saw you you had dark violet shadows under your eyes.
Your hair didn't have this gloss it has today.' He ran a
hand down its luxuriant, softly gleaming darkness.
'Now. . .' He scanned her face and smiled. 'Well, now
your eyes are shining and it's as though you're at home
inside yourself again.'

'And why?' she asked with passionate eagerness, then
answered herself. 'Because you helped to bring me back.
When you turned up here fresh from London—*my*
London—you seemed to prove that everything hadn't
ended. You talked to me about all the places I know—
Petticoat Lane and Camden Lock market, and the river,
and the lights on Albert Bridge. . .and the buskers and
the traffic—all the London things that I love. You
brought that part of my life back with you into this quiet
limbo up here. It seemed to prove that not everything
had come to an end. Some things that were important to
me were still going on.'

Ross tried to speak, but imperiously she halted him.

'No, wait. I haven't finished yet. At first I just thought
how kind you were. You didn't try to jolly me along.
You didn't talk about "taking me out of myself". But
you did talk to me. You ignored the way I behaved. You
seemed to see beyond it, to understand that I wasn't
being stand-offish and superior—just being the only way

I seemed capable of being. So, first you made me forget myself and answer you. Then tonight, when you kissed me, you brought me *back* to myself. Oh, Ross! Never say it shouldn't happen!'

'Not "shouldn't happen",' he said, his thoughtful eyes scanning her earnest face. 'Just "should have happened later"—if I'd only had the nous to hang on to my hormones more effectively.' His eyes crinkled in the way she found so devastatingly attractive as he grinned at his own words, and Zoë's newly awakened feelings swept through her.

'Oh, Ross! I do love you!' she said, her arms tightening around him again in a vice-like hug. Then, just as impulsively, she tore herself away from him and crouched down by the side of the rock, tearing at the grass and heather at its base.

He leaned over to watch. 'And what is my mature eighteen-year-old of the world doing now?'

'I want to see the bird you showed me. The one you carved when you were a boy.' She uncovered it, traced its spreading wings with her finger, then looked up at him. 'Ross—I would like you to carve another one. One for me. Because here was where we first realised we love each other. We do, don't we, Ross? It's not just me?'

He pulled her to her feet and crushed her against his chest.

'No, it's not just you, Zoë. From the moment I first saw you I've been holding you and kissing you like this in my imagination.'

'Then carve me that bird so that I've got something tangible to prove it. I shall need proof, Ross, tomorrow—to convince me I haven't been dreaming.'

He smiled with tender reassurance at her. 'You're not dreaming. And you shall have your bird, if I've not lost my old skill. When I carved that bird, you had scarcely opened your eyes on the world. Do you realise that?'

She laid a warning finger on his mouth to stop any further mention of the gap in their ages, and they began to walk down the hill to the point where their paths diverged—hers to Morag's cottage, his up again and over the dip in the skyline then down into remote Glen Innis where his family's dilapidated estate was.

'No sunset will ever be the same after this one,' Ross told her as they parted.

'Everything's going to be different. Everything!' She danced off over the rough grass to the corner of the cottage, where she stopped and watched him until he reached the crest of the hill and with one last wave of his hand disappeared from view.

Morag noticed the change in her at once. A distant, older cousin of Zoë's father, she had willingly opened her home to the grief-stricken Zoë after Charles Sutherland's death. He had sent a letter before he died, asking Morag to take his daughter under her wing for the first vulnerable months until she started her advanced secretarial course at Queen's College in London. Morag had instantly agreed—just as, years before, she had moved willingly to London when Zoë was a baby to take the place of the mother who lived barely long enough to see her daughter enter the world. Morag had provided the stable female presence in the Sutherland household until Zoë was old enough for them to manage without her, then, with as little fuss as she had made on arrival, she had quietly returned to her beloved Isle of Arran.

Now she looked fondly at the radiant face appearing in the cottage, remembering the sad little wraith she had met from the ferry almost three months ago at the start of the summer.

'You're looking well tonight,' she said with quiet satisfaction.

'It's your good Scottish air, Morag.' Zoë yawned ostentatiously. She didn't want to talk. Only to think of Ross. 'And it's making me sleepy too. I'll go up, I think.'

When she had had her bath she lay looking through the open lattice window at the sky, now deep purple-blue and studded with stars. She pictured herself and Ross in London—soon now, because she was due to go back in less than a week, and surely Ross's holiday must be almost over? They would have romantic suppers in each other's flats with long hours to be together without the watchful eyes of Ross's friends and neighbours observing them. Had he seen the Chelsea Physic Garden? Dined and danced on a Thames boat at night with the lights shimmering on the water? Seen the dawn from the high ground of the park at Richmond with the winding river glimmering through the morning mist far below?

Her dreams that night were peopled not with sad phantoms that made waking doubly painful, but with delicious dream adventures with Ross by her side. The future which her father's death had shattered so cruelly was there shining ahead of her again.

Ross must have gone up to the rock during the day while she was helping Morag at the shop she ran down on the shore, because when Zoë arrived there first the next evening, panting from her excited run up the hill, a second, smaller, brighter bird had joined the first, its outlines sharp against the mossy lower part of the stone seat. She was still down on her hands and knees looking at it and tracing the shape with her finger when Ross arrived.

'Is that what you wanted?' he asked.

'Exactly.' She scrambled to her feet and slid her arms round his neck. 'Thank you, Ross.'

The kiss was magic again. So she hadn't imagined it. Ross's words showed her that he felt the same.

'Tell me,' he said, breathing hard, laughing down at her, 'do you blend a little dynamite in that lipstick of yours?'

'Come and sit down.' She pulled him round to sit on the rock seat, and as his arm went into the familiar place round her shoulders she snuggled into the hollow of his neck, a spot that seemed designed specially for her. 'We've so much to talk about. I lay awake for ages last night thinking about what it's going to be like back in London. It won't be long now. Tuesday for me. When are you due back, Ross? You'll come and see me straight away, won't you? It's going to be a little hard there for me, just for a while, much though I want to be back in all the old familiar places. But with you——'

She looked up into his face at that point, and what she saw there cut short all the things she intended saying.

'What is it? Why are you looking like that?'

He took his arm away from her shoulders and got up, running a hand through his hair in what looked like frustration before turning to face her.

'Oh—damn it, Zoë. I don't believe this. How can you not know?'

'Know what?' Her voice was controlled, but her heart was beginning to thud with apprehension.

'What I'm going to do from now on. It never entered my head that you didn't know. It's been talked about loads of times among the crowd, and I know you were there.'

'I don't always tune in on what's going on. It's been like that rather a lot these last months.' Her blue eyes had darkened. 'You'd better tell me, if it's important enough to make you look like that.'

He sat down again and took her hands in his. 'You're cold.' He clasped them between his and rubbed them gently as he looked at her with a tenderness that frightened instead of reassuring her. 'Zoë—I'm not going back to London. I honestly thought you knew. I've made no attempt to keep it quiet.'

'Not going back?' Her world rocked again on its foundations for the second time that summer.

'I'm home for good from now on. To manage Innis Howe.'

'But—you're an economist. You belong in the City. What can you do up here in this backwater? London's all we've ever talked about.'

'You forget that before I was an economist I was a Macallister. I belong to Innis Howe. And if ever the place needed me it's now. The work's far beyond my parents, and the whole management needs rethinking if the estate isn't to go bankrupt.'

She seized eagerly on what seemed the obvious solution. 'So you'll rethink it, and then you'll come back to London. Well. . .that doesn't seem like the end of the world. I can survive if I can look forward to your coming.'

He was shaking his head. 'It's not a question of finding a quick solution and getting out. Innis Howe is my responsibility from now on. That's how it's got to be.'

She stared at him in raw, hurting disbelief. 'But that was before you—before I—before last night. Doesn't that alter anything?' She stumbled passionately over the words and her face, so bright and happy only moments ago, was pinched with the pain of what he was doing to her fragile hopes.

'Zoë, this just isn't something I can get out of—or,

indeed, want to get out of. My family's been at Innis
Howe for generations. A degree in economics and a bit
of time on the loose in London doesn't wipe that out.'

She pulled away from him angrily and leapt to her
feet, shoulders hunched against him, fists thrust into the
pockets of her mohair jacket.

'If you loved me, you'd come to London. I wouldn't
be so far down on your list of priorities.'

'If you think a little, you'll see that those words could
boomerang. I could tell you that if you loved me you'd
stay on Arran.'

She spun round. 'And give up college, and any chance
of the sort of job I want? Leave all the places I know and
love? The places I link with my father?' Her voice broke
on the words.

'If you loved me. . .' he said gently.

'The days are gone when a woman was expected to
give up everything for love,' she fired at him. 'Haven't I
lost enough, Ross? Must I lose everything? This place
isn't in my blood as you say it is in yours. As a matter of
fact I don't even like it. I've seen nothing of the world. I
don't want to bury myself away from it at the age of
eighteen. It's different for you. You've had your fling.'

'All of which adds up to what I was saying last night.
You're too young for what we allowed to happen.'

'Don't hide your own lack of enthusiasm behind my
lack of years,' she said fiercely. 'If you really cared about
me you'd want nothing more than to come to London to
look after me.'

'Your view of love is full of the romanticism of youth.
Love doesn't cancel out all other responsibility. It
doesn't write off all obligations to one's future children.
If I forsake Innis Howe, Zoë, I shall be depriving any
sons I may have of their own inheritance. Can't you
understand that?'

'Not really. I suppose it's because I'm as lacking in class as I am in years. Your upper-crust family loyalty is beyond me. You see, I've got such a limited family. None at all now, actually.'

Her voice was horribly bitter, and Ross gave a smothered exclamation. 'Oh—come here.' He tried to pull her towards him again, but she backed away. 'Don't look like that, Zoë. We can sort it out. You can have your time in London. There'll be long holidays and you can come and spend them all up here. There's time for more permanent plans when you're ready.'

'And if the estate can spare you, and the family, you'll throw the odd word in my direction—patronisingly, of course? It all sounds madly exciting.' She wanted to hurt him as much as he had hurt her. She felt she was fading away inside because of it. Twice in as many months a man she had thought central to her life had suddenly removed himself from the scene.

'Oh, Zoë! You're so——'

'Don't! Don't say that word again. And don't worry. I'm growing older every minute, thanks to experiences like the present one.' She looked with icy coldness at him. It was back again, the nothingness inside her, the total lack of feeling. 'You'd better find yourself a nice mature wee Scottish lassie,' she flung at him with heavy sarcasm. 'One who'll know her place from the word go.'

'Zoë!' His voice was angry, attempting to stop her. 'Don't rush off like this.'

'Goodbye, Ross,' she said without looking round, and kept on walking.

For Morag she made up some excuse about having phoned a friend and found that she was due to register at Queen's earlier than expected, so that she could legitimately leave on the early boat next day.

Morag went in to Brodick with her, knowing something was wrong, but sensing that Zoë did not want to be questioned.

'It will be better next time,' she told Zoë at the quayside, trying to convey her understanding of how hard the past months had been.

Zoë hugged her. 'Thank you for everything, Morag. But I doubt that there will be a next time up here for me. I wasn't born to island life as you were. I belong to London. But never think for a moment that I don't appreciate what you've done for me.'

'Ah, well. . .' Morag told her gently. 'We'll see.'

But Morag was destined not to see, though she never ceased adding to her letters the affectionate invitation, 'When are we to have you back at Innustulach again?' just as Zoë never failed to find good reasons for not accepting each invitation without ever giving the real one.

Ross sent letter after letter. She threw them away, and when they still came she started scrawling the return address and mailing them back to him.

Eventually the letters stopped. London and her course and new friends absorbed her. Later, work in France and again back in London filled her life to the exclusion of all thoughts of anywhere else. And Clive had come on the scene. . .

When Morag mentioned in one of her letters that Ross was married, Zoë thought, 'Good luck to him!' and carelessly screwed up the letter and threw it in the bin. Arran seemed very far away in both time and space, and very unimportant in the context of her busy life.

She wasn't conscious of the scar deep inside her covering the hurt she had suffered in the year of her eighteenth birthday. She prided herself on being less emotional, less impulsive now. Well and truly adult, in fact.

CHAPTER ONE

SADLY, what brought Zoë back to Arran was not the visit which would have so delighted Morag, but Morag's funeral five years after the summer of Charles Sutherland's death.

'I honestly can't think why you're bothering to go all that way,' Clive objected peevishly when she went into his office to tell him she simply had to have two days off. He was Clive Elliot of the wine importers Elliot and Chalmers, and she was due to leave with him on a buying tour of the French vineyards. Her decision to go to Morag's funeral would delay their departure, which was bad timing. If they had not been already rather more than employer-employee and promising to make further progress, he would have vetoed her journey without hesitation, she knew. 'Apart from anything else,' he went on more persuasively, 'if we're late setting off there'll be less time for Cannes at the end of the stint, and you know how much I was looking forward to that little interlude. I hoped you were, too.'

Zoë could guess the direction of his thoughts. He had already made several speculative forays around the subject of her moving in with him in a way that was not quite jokey, not quite serious—which was the story of Clive's attitude to life. Zoë was not over-enthusiastic about the 'live-in' scene. She found it rather disturbing that Clive only spoke of marriage—and other people's marriages at that—with faintly patronising amusement. Cannes would be their first holiday together. It might bring problems. But on the other hand it might well sort out her thoughts for her. Clive in many ways fitted her image of the ideal man. He was witty and sophisticated, and as caught up in London life as she was. She certainly had no wish to anger him.

'Is it worth it, my sweet?' he drawled, continuing to press her. 'After all, it isn't as though you've been haring off up there to see this Morag person while she was alive, is it? Not since I've known you, anyhow. And she's hardly in a position to get much out of this little effort right now, is she?'

Zoë smothered her dislike of the way he had expressed himself. 'I do realise that, Clive. But I owe it to her. She did a lot for me over the years.'

'No doubt she was well paid for it. Some kind of housekeeper, I think you said?'

'More than a housekeeper. Much more. I've got to go, Clive. I know how inconvenient it is just now, but I'll be back as quickly as I can. There really is no getting out of this one.'

The ferry was late leaving Ardrossan, and Zoë knew she would be hard-pressed to make it to Innistulach in time for the service, so she had a quick coffee in the refreshment bar before going to do her tidying-up in the ladies' room so that she would have no need to delay once they docked in Brodick. The boat was very busy, and after she had made sure that her glossy top-knot was anchored firmly and her make-up passed inspection she went out into the fresh air and made her way to the open deck area on the prow.

For a while she leaned on the rail watching as Arran grew out of the horizon and gradually shaped itself before her eyes.

Her conscience was uneasy, and as the island grew so did her feeling of guilt that she had not been back to see the living Morag. She should have done, she knew only too well. Nothing ought to have kept her away all these years. There was no real, justifiable excuse.

Restlessly she tore her eyes away from the purple hills and the proud blaze of colours on the flanks of Goat Fell, and began to walk towards the starboard deck, trying to find dulling of conscience in movement.

As she rounded the corner, she was aware of someone coming out of the doors of the refreshment room at the far end of the deck. He stood out because he was a tall, distinguished-looking figure in his dark suit against the almost uniform scruffy anoraks and jeans of the majority of passengers. After pausing to look out over the glistening water, he was beginning to turn to walk towards her, and she realised with a sharp indrawing of breath and a jolt that threatened to stop her heart that she was looking at Ross Macallister.

Blind panic gripped Zoë. She turned and hurried back round the corner to make for the port deck. He had just come out, she thought wildly as she almost ran along, so she must go in. She didn't want to meet him like this, unexpectedly. She had known that it was almost certain he would be at the funeral, but she would have keyed herself up to face him there. Now, stumbling across him like this, she was thrown completely off balance.

She looked back over her shoulder as she reached the starboard refreshment bar doors and was relieved to see no sign of Ross behind her. So it was another jolting shock when she realised that the man holding the door for her to enter was the very man she thought she had avoided. He must have seen her, guessed what she would do, and simply crossed the refreshment bar to make a fool of her.

'Good afternoon, Zoë,' he said in calm greeting. 'I

thought it was you. I see you haven't managed to work that tendency to bolt out of your system.'

'Ross. . .' she said weakly when she had managed to stop gaping at him. 'I didn't expect you to be on the boat.'

'Obviously. Nor did I expect to see you after so long. But here we are. In or out? We're blocking the doorway. I think outside is preferable.'

Zoë turned without speaking and took a couple of shaky steps to lean thankfully on the rail, needing its support but furious with herself for being so stupidly rocked on her foundations. Ross, his back against the rail, maddeningly relaxed, looked down at her.

'I take it you're here for Morag's funeral?'

'Of course.'

'Hardly "of course". I'm surprised you could fit it in. You haven't managed to see much of her in recent years, have you?'

He was voicing the thoughts that had been troubling her, but it was none of his business and she began to recover the power of speech.

'I know that, Ross. Don't imagine I'm not regretting it.'

He paused for a disapproving moment, then asked, 'Did you know she was in hospital?'

'No, I didn't.' At least she was not guilty on that score.

'An omission on someone's part. I thought most people who cared about her had been informed.' That was a nasty one. 'Still,' he went on, 'I don't suppose it would have made much difference. I'm sure you're a very busy person, and Arran is a long way from London.'

Zoë swallowed. 'I know you're only saying that to make me feel bad. There's no need to do that, Ross. I already feel bad enough.'

His jaw tightened grimly. 'But too late in the day for it to be of any use. Morag would have loved to see you. She talked of you constantly.'

'I wrote to her regularly.'

'The Post Office must have been glad of that.'

Zoë felt her hackles rise in spite of her guilt, and gathered strength. 'I work for my living, you know. And you really can't fit a trip up to this part of the world into a weekend.' She looked at him directly for the first time. 'In any case, Ross, since we're not mincing words, I think all that is between Morag and me, no matter what you feel.'

'And Morag won't be troubling you on the subject now, will she?' He saw the flash of pain in her eyes and waved a long-fingered hand dismissively. 'All right. I know your reluctance to face up to differences of opinion, especially when you might be hard put to it to justify your own position. But I do deeply resent any cavalier treatment of people I have a sense of responsibility for. And it isn't in my nature to let it pass without comment.'

'Don't worry. I've grasped that,' Zoë said with feeling. She gave him a scathing look. 'You're still very much the Lord of the Isle, I see.'

'Not at all. Merely a landowner who isn't content to regard the people who live on his land as nothing more than a source of income.'

There was not much that could be said in answer to that.

'I suppose you're going to the funeral?' Zoë said without much hope of a negative reply.

'I shall be there. I'd have been back on the last boat, but a meeting in Ardrossan went on longer than I'd anticipated.' He glanced ahead. 'We're almost there.'

Zoë seized her chance to get away. 'In that case I'll have a quick tidy-up before we're called to our cars.'

Ever punctiliously polite, Ross held the door for her to go into the bar, but gave her a brief nod and goodbye, remaining outside.

She made a second and unnecessary trip into the ladies' room, and lurked there, determined not to lay herself open to any further chance of having to talk to Ross Macallister. She had certainly not come too well out of that little encounter. She felt she'd had years of poise and experience steamrollered out of her. She stared at herself in the mirror, wondering what Ross had thought of her after the long lapse of time. Smooth, gleaming hair that had once been fly-away. Chic black jacket and fine black and white check skirt—simple, but smart. Immaculate white silk blouse that had cost a bomb. She pulled a face at the stupidity of her wonderings. What Ross thought of her had been evident in his words, and her appearance had nothing to do with his assessment. However, difficult though it had been she had at least got the first meeting over. There wouldn't be any need to speak to him again today, now.

The loudspeaker crackled into distinctly Scottish life, calling passengers to rejoin their cars, and Zoë warily emerged from her retreat, thankful to see no trace of a grey-suited, tall figure as she joined the file of passengers heading downstairs to the car deck.

She was delayed in driving off the boat once they docked in Brodick, as the car in front of her had starting problems so that its owner had to ferret around under the bonnet for a good ten minutes. So she had to put her foot hard down and roar across the String—the String Road, to give it its full name, which none of the locals ever did—to the far side of the island. Even so, she was late. There was a line of cars drawn up opposite the little

church on the shore at Innistraigh, but no people around.
Zoë could almost hear Morag's click of the tongue and
gently reproachful, 'Punctuality is the politeness of
kings, Zoë.'

'Sorry, Morag,' she said inwardly as she parked in the
only available space beside a large Range Rover. There
was no need to lock the car here, so she hurried straight
across and into the church without further delay, slipping into a back pew where there happened to be one of
the few empty seats.

She couldn't help being aware of Ross's broad
shoulders a little ahead of her across the aisle, his dark
hair burnished to a warm russet by the sunshine dazzling
through a window, but she looked quickly away from
him and straight ahead at the minister. Nothing but
Morag should fill her thoughts at this time. She concentrated on the service, and on her memories of the woman
for whom it was being held.

At the end of the sad little ceremony in the churchyard
people came up to Zoë, remembering her from her
original visit, including her in their grief for Morag with
simple, genuine friendship and a lack of reproach for her
long absence that paradoxically did nothing to reduce
her self-accusation.

She was taken aback for the second time that day
when she found herself confronted by Ross, her hand
clasped briefly in his as he expressed public sympathy
with her.

She thanked him, then added in a lower voice, 'No
need for a second session, Ross. We've done all this.'

'I understand how you feel,' he said with normal-
toned sympathy for the benefit of anyone listening, then
lowered his voice to add, 'But there's all the need in the
world for us to have a civil, publicly observed conversation. I love these people, but you know as well as I do,

Zoë, that they are watching us like hawks. There's nothing they'd enjoy more than a prolonged "Did you see Ross and Zoë ignoring each other?" session. I think you'll agree that the less of that nonsense the better.'

She found that by only the lightest of touches on her elbow he had manoeuvred her into leaving the churchyard at his side. The outcrop of rock on the coast meant that the church was a little way separate from the churchyard, so there was no getting away from Ross until they had covered that distance.

'And a walk in stony silence will do nothing at all to achieve our purpose,' he said smoothly. 'So how about saying something?'

'Since you're doing so well at organising everything, perhaps you'd like to choose a subject,' she said curtly.

'Certainly. Shall we begin with your left hand, which I see is conspicuously unadorned apart from what is obviously a dress ring on your middle finger? Does the whole of London contain no one to conform to your requirements? Are there no eligible bachelors these days?'

She allowed herself a superior little smile. 'It doesn't take a ring to mark a relationship, Ross.'

'It does in my book, quaint, old-fashioned fuddy-duddy that I am,' he said, looking as remote from his self-description as it was possible for him to be. 'Could it be that you are a little too exacting?'

'Not at all. I have a very full life—and a very satisfactory relationship,' she added defiantly, the defiance giving way to momentary bleakness at the empty sound of the words. She would have preferred to be able to match his marriage with a more demonstrable sign of her own satisfactory love-life, but that wasn't Clive's scene. However, she would show Ross that she didn't give a damn for the fact that he had married and she had not.

'I haven't had the chance to congratulate you on your own marriage, have I?' she asked him as they paused at the church wall. 'Morag told me about it, of course.'

'Rather old news now. It was some time ago,' he said, dismissing her congratulations as he caught the eye of a short, balding man who was hovering with patent desire to speak. 'Good afternoon, Duncan.'

'Good afternoon, Ross. A sad day. Innistraigh will miss Morag Kennedy. The shop won't be the same without her.'

'Nevertheless, she would want it to continue, whether she were here to go on running it or not. Have you met Zoë Sutherland?'

'Not yet. Though I have been waiting to do so.' He shook hands with Zoë. 'My sympathy, Miss Sutherland. Duncan Trease is the name. Miss Kennedy's solicitor. I'm sorry to intrude but I need to arrange to have a word with you.'

'In that case, I'll leave you,' Ross said, disappearing from Zoë's field of vision.

'Perhaps after the cup of tea I'm told they have prepared in the village hall we could find somewhere to have a more serious, quiet word?' Duncan Trease went on, losing no time.

Zoë turned and saw for the first time the new building that had been added behind the church since her last visit to Innistraigh. She decided instantly that tea and chat were the last things she wanted, in public at least. She definitely had no desire to bump into Ross again.

'I think I'll opt out of that,' she told the solicitor. 'I'll make my way up to Morag's cottage. Perhaps you'll join me there in about half an hour? I can do with a little breathing-space.'

She gave him no time to protest, just smiled dismissively and crossed the road to her car. Let the local people say what they liked about her absence. She was not up to facing that hall and Ross's condemning grey eyes again.

She had only got as far as putting out her hand to open the car door when a voice stopped her.

'Not staying to tea, Zoë?'

Ross was watching her from the open window of the Range Rover, so she had not escaped him after all, merely walked right into him again. She smothered an exasperated sigh.

'No. I'm tired. It's a long drive from London in one go.'

He got out of the Range Rover again, innate courtesy stopping him from remaining seated when she was standing, and stood dwarfing her with his broad-shouldered presence.

'I can't say that I ever find the obligatory get-together after these sad occasions at all appropriate, but people seem to feel it must be done.' He looked along the shore towards Morag's shop, his clear grey eyes thoughtful. 'Duncan was right. This place will miss Morag. She's kept that shop going in the face of all odds—and I suspect at cost to herself.' His eyes focused on her again. 'But I mustn't bore you. I remember that you had little patience with our desire to cling to continuity. Little liking for Arran, come to that.'

Zoë shrugged. 'I was too young to know what I liked in those days. This afternoon, from the prow of the boat, I thought the island looked absolutely lovely. I had to race across against the clock, but even so I still had time to appreciate how idyllic Glen Shiskine is.'

'You even remember the name. I'm rather surprised.'

'And the names of the villages. Machrie and Auchencan. Dougarie and Imachar. They have a kind of rhythm. I always liked them.'

He seemed to realise that they had been in danger of talking normally, and changed his tone. 'Will you be staying at one of the hotels, or slumming it at the cottage?'

Zoë's hackles rose. 'Anyone who refers to Morag's immaculate, welcoming cottage as a place where one "slums it" does her a gross injustice,' she said sharply.

He raised his eyebrows. 'I was thinking more in terms of your opinion than my own. As an incomer from bright lights and sophistication, that is.'

'You were being offensive.'

'I assure you I meant no disrespect. . .to Morag,' he added with perfect punch timing. 'But you didn't answer my question. Innistulach, or elsewhere?'

'Innistulach,' she said shortly. 'I wouldn't dream of going anywhere else.'

He looked assessingly at her for a moment, then asked abruptly, 'Why did you come? It would have been far easier to write off this place. You'd more or less done that.'

'But I hadn't written off Morag, whatever you may think,' she said emphatically, angry to hear the constriction of threatening tears in her voice. She wouldn't cry in front of him. She *wouldn't*!

'And Duncan wants to speak to you, so at least you'll have privacy. Perhaps you'll find the journey has been worthwhile.'

That was the last straw.

'Bastard!' she fired at him, surprising herself by the vehemence of the word she had uttered, but not him. It bounced off him like a midge off an elephant.

'Hardly that. I have the strongest family connections,

as I would have thought you'd good reason to remember. Once again you misunderstand me. I merely meant that there may be some small keepsake for you in the terms of Morag's will.'

'If that is so, I shall treasure it for her sake.'

'I'm sure you will. You can keep it with her letters. A distant reminder—since that's the sort of connection you seem to prefer.'

'That's enough, Ross.' Choked with hurt and anger, Zoë slammed into her car, but he snatched the door open again.

'When you do speak to Duncan Trease, think carefully about what he has to say to you.'

She hadn't the remotest idea what he was talking about, and she had no desire to find out. Zoë switched on the engine and practically forced the accelerator through the floorboard of her little Mini.

'Is there anything that happens on this island that you don't feel the urge to inferfere with?' she shot at him venomously.

His answer was quite calm and matter-of-fact. 'Not much.' He closed the door smartly before taking a long-legged stride up into the Range Rover.

Zoë drove off, but once she had seen the Range Rover turn northwards she slammed on her brakes and parked so that she could close her eyes and resort to yoga breathing to calm herself down. She didn't feel fit to handle a lethal vehicle even on these quiet roads until she had regained control of herself.

She had come up here to mourn Morag, and at every turn she had been distracted from doing so by Ross Macallister, for whom accusation seemed to take precedence over mourning. She had wanted it to be a thoughtful, quiet day, and instead it had been full of hostility and unpleasantness. With an effort she banished thoughts of Ross from her mind and concentrated on her measured breathing. Gradually she grew less aware of the pounding of her blood, and more conscious of the quiet lap of the waves on the pebbles of the shore. She remembered that Morag had collected enough of the larger stones in soft browns and greys to build a fireplace with them, and as she remembered the fireplace and its owner the calming-down process was complete and she could switch on the engine again.

Morag's little general store at the other end of Innistraigh from the church had been shuttered when Zoë drove past earlier. Now it was open, its blinds bright above the windows to keep the sun off the goods displayed. So someone was holding the fort—but for how long?

Zoë pulled into the parking space and went over for milk and bread to take up to the cottage, sure that Morag's store cupboard would supply anything else she needed. She had an ulterior motive. She was curious to find out who was running the shop, and whether the arrangement was long term.

There was no one there as she walked through the door, the delicately balanced little bell tinkling a confirmation of her footsteps, but a girl of her own age with light brown curly hair and a sprinkling of golden freckles came through from the back, fastening a white coat. Zoë recognised her at once.

'Fiona Kerr!' she said.

'Fiona Bayne now,' the girl smilingly corrected. 'Alec and I were married last year. Remember him? How are you, Zoë? I saw you at the church, but I didn't hang around after the service. I came straight back here and started up the action again. I seemed to hear Morag saying we'd wasted enough good opening hours! She wouldn't have wanted anyone to be inconvenienced, even by her own funeral.'

'So you're running the shop,' Zoë said, when Fiona had got the milk out of the cold counter.

'Morag asked me to take over when she went into hospital. She never stopping thinking and worrying about the place.' Fiona's hazel eyes looked warmly into Zoë's. 'She'd have been glad you came today. Relieved, too, that you're here to sort things out. To be perfectly honest, I never thought we should see you on Arran again, Zoë.'

The five-years-gone summer and its misery flooded back into Zoë's mind, but this time she could speak of it. Wanted to, she was a little surprised to realise. The sight of Fiona's warm, pretty face made her want to explain her own stand-offishness throughout the weeks when they first knew each other.

'I owe you an apology for the way I behaved towards you all that summer,' she said impulsively. 'You were so kind, and I gave you all the cold shoulder.'

'I don't know about all. . . There was Ross!' Fiona smiled. 'Oh, forget it, Zoë. You had every excuse with your father just dying. Who wouldn't have felt unhappy? We understood.'

'It wasn't just the fact that he'd died,' Zoë said determinedly. 'I made Morag swear not to tell anyone the real truth, and knowing her I don't suppose she ever did. My father committed suicide, Fiona. Rationally, calmly, and as much for my sake as anything. That was what I couldn't take.'

'No!' Fiona's face contorted with shock. 'I never dreamed——Oh, that's awful, Zoë. And you had no mother to help you cope.'

'My mother was another contributory factor. She'd died of inoperable cancer soon after I was born. And that was what he found out he'd got. He said in his letter he left me that he wouldn't inflict the sad months he went through with my mother on anyone, and he assured me that what he had done was the best way for both of us. I think now that he was very brave, and—in the light of his own experience—probably quite certain he was doing the right thing. But *then* I felt that he'd made me to a great extent responsible for his death. It twisted my thinking on everything. I wasn't old enough to cope, that's the short answer.' She picked up the milk. 'But that's enough of that. It's a long time ago. I just felt that you deserved an explanation of my attitude.'

'I'm sorry it was such a sad one—and I do understand.' Fiona squeezed Zoë's arm, then went along with the change of conversation. 'So—what have you been doing all this time?'

'Getting myself good secretarial qualifications which I've never used—though they did open the door to the kind of job I wanted. And after that a year's interpreter's course in French—which I do use a lot in my present job.'

'And what's that?'

'I work for Elliot and Chalmers. They're wine importers, with their head office and premises just off Pall Mall. We buy a lot from France, of course, and I tend to be trouble-shooter on those trips.'

Fiona grinned. 'Sounds a bit more exotic than "half a pound of Golden Cow and a quarter of cheese".' She looked, as Ross had done, at Zoë's left hand. 'Still fancy-free? Not hooked Mr Elliot or Mr Chalmers?'

'Mr Chalmers is rather a grandfather. Mr Elliot——' Zoë wiggled her fingers to convey indecision. 'Maybe, maybe not. It's early days.'

Fiona followed her to the door. 'Did you get the

chance of a word with Ross?' It was quite obviously not
a *non sequitur*.

'Just a brief one.'

'You know he's married?'

'Morag told me in one of her letters.'

'Funny how things turn out. We were all busy that
summer planning quite a different future for him. We
all thought that you and he——'

'It was a long time ago,' Zoë repeated firmly. 'I was only
a kid, and not quite in my right mind. I must be off now,
Fiona. I'll see you again once I've spoken to Morag's
solicitor and let you know what's going to happen.'

'You'll see me tonight if you look out of the cottage
window,' Fiona said. 'Alec and I have Mum and Dad's
old place at Innistulach. They moved to a bungalow in
Whiting Bay when we got married.'

'See you later, then, maybe.'

The track elbowed back on itself twice in the steep climb
up to Innistulach, Zoë remembered. But then she had
been climbing on foot. This time it was far more hair-
raising with the car wheels slithering noisily on the rough
stones loosened from their uneven bed by a month of
unusual heat and dryness.

Two dark specks in the sky over the hilltop caught
Zoë's eye, making her slow down. The golden eagles.
The leisurely arc and poise of their flight identified them,
even at this distance.

She speeded up again, turning eventually into the
farmyard around which the three remaining Innistulach
properties clustered. The farm house—Fiona's now—
had been rebuilt with more height and bedrooms over
the same ground area, but there was a familiar breed of
pig rearing up against the sheet of corrugated iron
blocking the doorway of its sty.

Morag's cottage was just as it had always been. Uneven white stone walls, low grey slate roof housing, unbelievably, an upstairs where it seemed impossible for there to be one, roses climbing round the door. . .and the whole cottage seeming to shoulder companionably into the hillside for protection.

Zoë had forgotten about the little matter of a key, but it was rare for doors to be locked, she remembered, and sure enough the heavy door opened easily on to the stone-flagged hall.

Leaving her luggage, Zoë walked into the remembered scent of rose pot-pourri. She went into the little sitting-room, up two steps to the left. Morag's patchwork knitting bag was leaning against her chair, a tiny baby jacket which would never now be finished on the needles. It was little things like that that brought home to you the finality of someone's death, Zoë thought, swallowing the lump that had suddenly grown in her throat.

The little row of ornaments on the fireplace were all reminders of friends and charges from Morag's past. Among them was the glass paperweight Zoë herself had chosen as a parting gift when she grew too old for Morag's presence in their London flat to be necessary, and she could remember vividly the conflict of emotions she had felt on that occasion—proud desire for independence warring with sadness at parting with Morag's stable female presence.

Zoë went through to the kitchen at the other end of the cottage and filled the kettle. Someone had been in to tidy around, because there were no stale odds and ends of loaves in the bread bin. While she waited for the kettle to boil, she went up the narrow twisting stairs to the two bedrooms and upstairs sitting-room looking out across the rising hillside. She had slept in the room to the left at the top of the stairs, and she went in there now to open the window in the roof and let in fresh air.

'Your bed is waiting,' Morag had always said at the end of her letters, and it was waiting now—not an unused-looking guest room bed with folded blankets and lumpy top cover, but fresh and lavender-scented, its flower-sprigged sheets topped with a plump duvet. Zoë took off her jacket and tossed it on the bed, the lump back in her throat.

'Miss Sutherland?' She recognised the deep voice of Duncan Trease calling up the stairs, and ran down to find him in the hall.

'Go into the sitting-room, Mr Trease,' she told him. 'I'll bring in the tea things. I'm sure you'll manage another cup.'

And so, in all innocence, prepared to hear of some personal bequest, Zoë came back with tea and a rich fruit cake she had found foil-wrapped in a cupboard.

By the time Duncan Trease left, her head was reeling with the implications of the terms of Morag's will. The cousin who should have inherited, according to Zoë's knowledge of the family, had died before Morag, and the new will left the cottage to herself—but with conditions that she could see were either going to complicate her life enormously or leave her with a mega-huge permanent sense of guilt.

If she accepted the cottage, she was to accept also responsibility for ensuring that the shop went on functioning as such, backed by the income from a studio flat adjoining it, which Morag also owned. Every future change of tenant of the shop was to be arranged and masterminded by Zoë—*ad infinitum*.

Why had Morag done this—knowing as she did that Zoë had no fondness for Arran and was patently reluctant to visit the place?

If she couldn't accept the responsibilities laid down, the will went on to specify, then cottage, shop and studio flat were to be sold and the proceeds used for the benefit of the people of Innistraigh with the proviso that the shop should be sold to someone committed to running it as such. That condition, however, could only be enforced for the first sale, Mr Trease pointed out, so indirectly Zoë could be responsible for the little community losing its vital local source of supplies.

'It's blackmail!' she burst out as Duncan Trease looked up at her.

He looked mildly shocked. 'Hardly blackmail. Gentle persuasion. Surely no more than that?'

'You think so?' she said sceptically. 'Morag knew that I'd a sense of responsibility that she made sure she instilled in me from age nought to fifteen. She was always a past master of the iron hand in the velvet glove.'

'But I'm sure she was thinking of the best for everyone—not least yourself. Read this sub-clause.'

He handed the will to her, and Zoë could almost hear Morag's voice as she read the very personal words he indicated.

I am very well aware that Zoë Sutherland may view the cottage as a liability and the need to deal with the shop's affairs as an unwanted chore. I earnestly beg her to accept the latter in memory of me as a service to the community which I have loved, a service which enables a small business on which the more fragile members of that community depend to survive. If she does this, I hope that the cottage will bring her, as often as she uses it, the happiness I have myself found within its walls. I hope too that it will lead her to love a place that will return love with peace and tranquillity, qualities which may be lacking in her present life.

She had been almost moved to tears as she read those words, but after Mr Trease had gone Zoë felt overwhelmed. Peace and tranquillity! she thought frustratedly, looking down at the solicitor's card which he had left with her so that she could consider her decision and phone him when she had reached it.

As though on cue, the phone rang, and when she picked it up she was instantly, blisteringly aware of the further complication that any involvement with Arran would bring.

'Just a brief query. . .' Ross began. 'It occurred to me that you could find yourself without the ingredients of a square meal since the cottage has been empty for a week or two now and the shop will have closed a few minutes ago.'

Zoë scowled. 'Concern over my welfare is a bit of a change of tune, isn't it?'

'You are a guest on the island.'

'Don't blame me for thinking that so far you seem to have considered me an unwelcome one.'

'As a Scot, I care for the welfare of every guest,' he said in a tone that implied that only a savage would think otherwise. 'All the same, I think we both feel that an invitation to dinner at Innis Howe would be inappropriate.'

'It certainly would,' Zoë said with feeling.

'But a freezer meal, if it would help, could be delivered to the cottage within half an hour, at no inconvenience or embarrassment to anyone.'

He had the knack of being so damnably decent even while he was being offensive.'

'Thanks for the offer, but everything is taken care of,' she said grudgingly.

'Then that's fine. Duncan's gone?'

She remembered with a deepening of the frown on her

forehead that Ross had seemed to know something was in the air for her when the meeting with Morag's solicitor was fixed. How on earth was he involved in it? The grand octopus with a tentacle in every pond? Well—she wasn't going to get involved in an interrogation about her intentions until she knew them herself. And not then either, if she could help it.

'Yes. Oh! Something's boiling over. Must go. Thanks for calling.' She put the phone down thankfully and turned to find a marmalade cat sitting behind her, staring up at her with round, almond-green eyes. 'Polly?' she said questioningly. The cat stood and stretched, then, tail erect, took a step towards her. Zoë crouched down, feeling for the name tag on the collar. Yes—it was Polly, who must be every day of fourteen years old now. Morag's cat. 'Have I inherited you as well?' she asked. 'Or have you transferred your allegiance to whoever has been feeding you?' She sat on the stairs and Polly jumped on to her lap. An absent-minded stroking session brought Zoë a small measure of comfort—but not enough.

She had come back to Arran for a duty visit, and she seemed now to be in danger of taking on a lifetime's responsibility. Hypothetically, she could find herself with a cat, a cottage and a business to keep going. And Ross only too ready to put her right at every turn.

On the other hand, thinking with cold self-interest, the cottage could be locked and left forever if need be, if no one bought it. The shop could take its chance—and whoever had been feeding Polly could go on doing so.

She sighed. Already it seemed quite impossible to think along those lines. Maybe Fiona would carry on running the shop, and that would solve the immediate problem. If she couldn't do that, Zoë realised with a further sinking of the heart, it would take much more time than she had bargained for when she told Clive that their trip wouldn't be long delayed.

Clive! She jumped up, pouring Polly off her lap. She had promised to ring him much earlier than this.

All the same, she hesitated before dialling his number. Clive seemed to be a not very solid figure, diminished in her awareness by too many meetings with Ross Macallister. She was suddenly nervous about Clive. Not about speaking to him, but about the very fact of him.

She dialled, telling herself to get on with it. But, as she waited for him to answer, Ross's voice, so decisive and so recently heard, was the one her ear seemed to expect. When Clive spoke, his light drawl was almost a surprise.

CHAPTER TWO

'SCRAP the damned lot, for heaven's sake!' Clive's opinion was instant. 'What's the use of a holiday cottage at the back of beyond—and one shrouded in Scottish mist to boot? If it comes with a load of other troubles attached to it you'll be far better off without it.' There was a little silence, then an afterthought. 'How much of a turnover is there at the shop?'

'Just enough to keep it going, I imagine. In a good year, that is. The income from the flat is tied up to act as buffer for the bad years.'

Clive made a sound of disgust. 'What did I tell you? Forget it, Zoë. Let them sell the lot.'

Zoë found protest at his riding-roughshod attitude rising in her. 'It isn't just a matter of the profit. A lot of people depend on this little shop. It's all that stands between them and a six-mile walk in either direction to the next source of supplies.'

'Oh—rubbish, sweetie. They can get in their cars and turn the ignition key, surely? Don't go all straight-faced and responsible on me.'

'They don't all have cars. This isn't a London suburb, Clive. And if it's a question of depriving them of one of their few amenities then it *is* a responsibility.'

'More so than your job, apparently. Or than any serious interest in the time we're due to spend together, it seems to me. Aren't you rather trading on our relationship, darling?' The 'darling' was icy, and about as far from an endearment as anything could be. But he had a point.

Zoë sighed and her voice softened to a more conciliatory tone. 'I do care about the inconvenience—and about
the disappointment. Really I do. But this thing has
happened and involved me. I can't ignore it. I'm just
going to have to stay on a day or two longer to sort it
out.'

'And if it takes more than a day or two?'

'It won't. I won't let it.' Zoë spoke with more confidence than she felt. 'I really am sorry, Clive. I'll hope to
have news for you tomorrow.'

'For which small mercy I must be thankful?' But his
voice had thawed again. 'Anyway, you're too far away
for me to do what I would most like and drag you back
forcibly again. Besides which, I have things to do and
people to see. So on your misguided way with you,
sweetie. But not too far in the wrong direction, I must
warn you. I am not a man of infinite patience.'

Ruffled by the call, Zoë went up to the first-floor
sitting-room—originally a large landing, but with too
good a view to waste and plenty of room for a settee and
comfortable chairs. She sat for a long time in the chair
by the window, watching the sun go down over the
Sound. The red glow spread along the horizon until the
hills of Kintyre were silhouetted against its fire, then
slowly it faded and the sky overhead darkened to a
velvety royal blue against which the first of the stars and
a thin sliver of moon shone and mirrored themselves in
the still, shining water. She felt better for watching it, as
though the scene had been painted over her own worries
and irritations, obliterating them.

Tomorrow she would tackle Fiona. But now she was
going to make herself a cheese omelette and have thick
slices of the crusty loaf from the island bakery via
Morag's shop. Then bed. She smothered a yawn and

made her way down to the dark kitchen, switching on lights. The day had been eventful enough.

'I wish I could stay on, but this was only a temporary arrangement, we thought, to see Morag over a bad time,' Fiona said regretfully when Zoë caught her at a quiet moment in the shop next morning. 'You see—I've promised most of the summer to the Bell Rock in Blackwaterfoot. Their receptionist is going on maternity leave for the rest of the summer. I can't let them down now that I've given my word.'

'Of course you can't. It's just that it would have been so convenient to settle things quickly—which my boss is all too keen for me to do.' Zoë explained briefly about the French trip.

'Well. . .if you're not bothered about having loads of applicants to select from, I think I know someone who'd jump at the chance to run Morag's,' Fiona said diffidently. 'She helped a bit here over Easter, actually, while she was staying with me. And she's got good reason for wanting to get out of Glasgow.'

'I'd welcome any help you can come up with,' Zoë said with feeling.

'In that case, she's a cousin of mine. A widow, juggling an unsuitable job and a small child with the usual problem of how to afford anything on one income. If she could have a bit of a wage and the upstairs of this place to live in, she'd jump at it, I'll lay any bet.'

'Live here? You mean the holiday flat next door?'

'No. Upstairs. Morag did, the past two winters, to save herself the haul up to Innistulach. It's quite cosy. And Innistraigh school would be wonderful for my cousin's child. So do you want me to sound Catriona out? I wouldn't suggest her if I didn't know she was well worth a try.'

Zoë accepted the offer with alacrity, and five minutes later she had an appointment to go over to Glasgow next day on the first ferry and meet Fiona's cousin.

'I'm so grateful,' she told Fiona. 'If I can ever do anything for you——'

'You can, actually!' Fiona grinned as she seized her chance. 'This afternoon, if you're not too busy. There's a "do" in Lamlash that Alec and I have to go to this evening, and look at this mess!' She ran her hands through her curly hair. 'If you could take over for the last couple of hours from four, I could get it done by someone who'll make a better job of it than I should after closing-time.'

Zoë agreed willingly, and Fiona pointed out a folder under the counter.

'It would kill two birds with one stone as a matter of fact. You won't be rushed off your feet so you could have a look at these papers between customers. They're details of things Morag ordered—a whole spate of them in the last week before she went into hospital. I can't think why she did it at that point—just adding to her problems. Everything's paid for in advance or it might have been worth trying to cancel some of them. But nobody will want to hand back good money, will they?'

A customer came in and Zoë left, feeling considerably more optimistic than when she entered the shop. She took the short cut up through the tiny wood and fields where someone's Highland Cattle were grazing, gentle eyes peering through shaggy long hair. There was a thick carpet of bluebells under the trees, dazzling under the tender green of the leaves, and she picked a few for the window-sill in the sitting-room, so it turned out not to be such a short cut after all.

She felt very relaxed and happy—and she hadn't thought of Ross Macallister once—unless thinking that you were not thinking about someone counted adversely. Maddeningly, now that he was in her mind, if only in a negative way, he hovered around as though just out of sight, and she found herself looking about warily as she approached the three cottages, but there was no one waiting there. Why should there be? There were only the hens scratching for insects in the dust, and Fiona's and Alec's pig grunting inquisitively from the shadowy interior of its sty.

She relaxed again too soon. As though she had called him up by her thoughts, the phone rang as soon as she entered the cottage and Ross's voice said, 'Zoë? Just a quick word.'

Her heart had reacted to the sight of him yesterday, and now her legs seemed to lose all strength at the sound of his deep voice with its faint trace of Scottish accent. She subsided on to the bottom step of the stairs, holding the phone as though it were a snake.

'Yes? You've only just caught me. I've been down to the shop.'

'I won't keep you long. I take it that you're in the picture as far as the cottage is concerned now that you've spoken to Trease?'

'I am,' she said uncommunicatively.

'Then there are one or two things I would like to see to while you're here.'

'Just a minute, Ross. How much do you know about Morag's will? I would have expected it to be a private matter between her and her solicitor, not common knowledge.'

'She asked my advice about it. As I'm Feu Superior she knew that I would obviously be concerned about what happened to property on Macallister land.'

'So I have you to thank for the predicament I'm in now? Thanks very much!' Zoë said with feeling.

'Don't be ridiculous. Of course I had nothing to do with any bequests Morag wanted to make. I merely discussed safeguards for the property whichever of the options laid down in the will was taken up. Don't worry—it was Morag's wish, and only Morag's, that you should be involved.'

And that was a bucket of cold water if anything was.

'So what do you want to talk to me about?' Zoë said, quickly changing the subject.

'Two things. First, it's time for the annual check on the property and if you're going to be in later this afternoon I could call in around five to get it done then.'

'Sorry. I'm out then.' She was not at all sorry. She didn't want to see Ross again. 'I think there's a key at Fiona's, though.'

'Never mind about that. I'll arrange something. The second thing is that Morag had asked for one of the estate carpenters to do some shelf-fitting at the shop. He's not got much on at the moment. If it's still on the cards, I'd like it to be in the next couple of weeks.'

'You expect me to have found out quite a lot in the short time I've been here,' Zoë said aggrievedly.

'You're going to have to, aren't you? And since I don't imagine you'll want to miss out on too much of that fascinatingly busy life in London I supposed you'd want to do it as quickly as possible. I'm only trying to help.'

Like hell you are, Zoë thought. You're just throwing your weight around—but, whatever she felt about it, on the surface of it he was doing the shop a favour.

'I shall be down at the shop this afternoon from four onwards,' she said. 'If the carpenter could call in then, I shall know more about it. I know there are papers about goods ordered.'

'Right. He'll do that. That's all, then.' The phone

clicked into abrupt silence then the dialling tone buzzed in her ear. Zoë pulled a face at it and put it down.

She prepared a beef casserole with the beef she had brought back from the shop—more than she would eat tonight, but it would be something to have tomorrow when she got back from Glasgow. She took a sandwich lunch up the hill, and Polly came with her, bright gold against the heather. There was so much toing and froing on the Sound to watch that Zoë almost forgot the time and had to do a dash down the track in the car to avoid being late at the shop.

There was a spasmodic trickle of customers when Fiona had gone. A little bustle of children from the junior school filled the shop with bright, burred voices and careful negotiations to make a few pence go as far as possible until four-thirty, then, apart from three or four groups of holiday-makers wanting chocolate and cold drinks there was a quiet spell.

Zoë looked through Morag's orders. There was apparently a new cold cabinet on its way, plus what seemed like rather a lot of shelving due for delivery within the next few days, so that would fit in with Ross's carpenter's availability.

She mooched around the shop, mentally rearranging it, planning an outside café area, for which there was ample space. The carpenter came in as arranged, introducing himself as Donald from Machrie.

'A couple of days should see it done, once they deliver,' he told Zoë. 'One day to get the old stuff out, another to put the new in. If you ring the estate office— here's a card with the number—Mr Macallister will let me know.'

'It won't be me. I'll be back in London long before that,' Zoë told him firmly. 'But someone will get in touch.'

'Fine. Whoever, as long as we know. By the way—
mind you lock up securely tonight. There's been one or
two break-ins over Brodick way, my brother in the police
told me. You never know whether they'll try their luck
over here.'

'I thought there was no crime on Arran!'

He grinned. 'There was even a bad wee snake in the
Garden of Eden, remember. Just take care.'

At a quarter-past five, Miss Ward from the third
Innistulach cottage came in for a sizeable order that kept
Zoë weighing and calculating and trying to talk about
the future of the shop at the same time.

While she was below counter level putting the bacon
back, the shop bell tinkled again and Zoë saw through
the glass of the cold cabinet that Ross Macallister had
come in.

'We have a new shop lady today, Mr Macallister,'
Miss Ward said brightly.

'We have indeed, Miss Ward. Will she do, do you
think?'

'Oh, very nicely, I'm sure.'

'Brings that touch of sophistication to our wee store,
doesn't she?'

While the mild banter was exchanged, Ross's eyes
were watching Zoë as she weighed a pound of Arran
Pilots, turning her fingers into thumbs and making her
overshoot the bag so that a fusillade of potatoes went all
over the floor and she had to start weighing all over
again.

Once more it had happened—that sudden electric
stinging feeling that tightened her chest and made her
have to think where the next breath was coming from.

He was wearing fawn cords tucked into knee-high
leather boots that were polished like burnished conkers,
and an olive-green ribbed sweater over an open-necked

white shirt, the collar turned back and the cuffs of which contrasted with the outdoor tan of his neck and arms. Zoë could feel his grey eyes on her all the time as she retrieved the potatoes from the floor behind the counter, something she was doing more to give herself time to calm down than for any other reason. It was crazy that she should feel like this. Quite incomprehensible. She took a couple of deep breaths and stood up again.

'Will that be all, Miss Ward?'

'It will indeed.' Miss Ward, old as she was, was undeniably flirting with Ross as he helped to stow her groceries in the worn leather shopping-bag. Zoë thought for a moment what a lovely picture they made, the tiny silver-haired lady with the faded eyes and the tall, muscular man stooping protectively over her, his rich brown hair contrasting so vitally with hers as he fitted the last packet into the bag she was holding open.

'There we are. All present and correct.' Ross caught Zoë's eyes on him, and she snapped out of her reverie.

'That's a very heavy bag, Miss Ward,' she said.

'Not at all. I'm used to it.' The old lady moved it, not without difficulty, to the edge of the counter.

Zoë realised that she was about to be left alone in the shop with Ross, and she didn't fancy the idea.

'Look—I'll be going up the hill in a few minutes. If you'd like to wait until I've served Mr Macallister, I'll give you a lift. You really shouldn't be struggling up that climb with such a heavy load.'

Miss Ward swung the bag off the counter with surprising speed. 'Indeed? The day I can't manage my own messages is not here yet, Miss Sutherland. I'll be fine. Thank you for your kind thought. Good afternoon to you both.'

Ramrod-stiff, she left the shop with Zoë staring,

puzzled, after her while Ross closed the door behind the apparently offended back.

'What did I do wrong there?' she asked, forgetting her awkwardness with Ross.

'Something it's only too easy for a Southerner to do. You haven't a clue how we islanders tick.'

Zoë bridled at the patronising note she detected in his tone, and the colour flooded into her face under his level gaze.

Her chin lifted defiantly. 'But you, no doubt, are ready to educate me on the subject.'

'You asked a question. I was about to answer it.' He was so smoothly matter-of-fact that her hackles rose even more.

'And of course you're among the best-qualified to explain anything to do with Arran, having spent most of your life at school and university and work on the mainland. How many years was it? Twenty-one out of twenty-eight when I last knew you spent away from here? I should have thought that length of time would have ironed all the native Scot out of you.'

'Dear me—you are ruffled, aren't you, Zoë?' he said with infuriating calm. 'But all you are dong is demonstrating your lack of understanding with every word. Do you really think that being away from here can do away with generations of genetic inheritance? This place is in me. . .and the ways of its people. And always will be.'

'Well,' she said dismissively, 'either you're going to put me right or you're not. My money's on your not being able to resist the temptation.' She picked up a cloth and began to wipe the counter busily.

'True. What Scot misses a chance to educate the uninformed?' He unhurriedly stood up a pile of boxes of chocolates that she had knocked over, then in one swift move stopped her hand with its cloth and pinned it on the counter between them with his own. 'I like my words of wisdom to be listened to, so do me the courtesy of stopping that nonsense for a moment. What you did was right in intent, wrong in execution. Miss Ward can do with help. She knows it, but she doesn't like to be made aware of it by other people. It's a matter of preserving her illusion of independence. If you had made her feel she was doing you a favour by accepting a lift up to Innistulach, it would have had a completely different effect.'

Zoë, conscious of the pressure of his hand, twice as big as her own, warm when hers through nervousness was clammy cold, wriggled her fingers free and stuck them in the pocket of the white coat she had borrowed from Fiona.

'If you're saying that to get by here you have to weigh every word and talk in riddles, then I can't be doing with that.'

'We like plain speech too, but did Morag never drum into you "Think before you speak"?'

'Resorting to clichés, Ross? Dear me!'

'There's a wealth of truth in them.'

She gave a superior little smile. 'I think I can speak the truth. But I prefer to do it with a measure of originality.'

'As I remember it, you're an expert at saying nothing at all.'

The past flowered instantly at his words, so that time seemed to have gone into reverse. Her refusal to see him again once she knew he was not returning to London, to even read one of his letters, flared like a banner between them. With an enormous effort Zoë tore her eyes away from the unwavering accusation in his and tried to defuse the situation.

'So—we differ,' she said lightly. 'But it's getting late.

I'm sure you came in for some genuine reason. What can I do for you, Ross?'

He went along with her efforts. 'My *Financial Times*. It's over on the right there with my name on it.'

Zoë handed it to him and took payment. 'I'm surprised you still read it,' she said. 'I thought you'd given all that up in favour of Innis Howe.'

Ross tucked the paper under his arm. 'I'll top up your education on one other matter before I go,' he said. 'The world doesn't stop turning beyond the limits of the London Underground. We elect a Member of Parliament. We follow the news. Sometimes we even, in our modest way, make it. In short, we are part of the world, Zoë. End of lesson—and goodnight!' The shop bell rang as he opened the door and went out.

Zoë was left feeling a distinct lack of pride in herself. She had behaved, on the whole, like a gauche if not downright unpleasant schoolgirl. This encounter had been more difficult than the last. It wasn't easy for either of them but surely two grown people could manage to forget the boy-and-girl affair they had had when they met up again?

She was glad that it was almost six. She could put up the sunblinds and get away any minute now—and boy!—was she ready for that.

She ran into trouble again outside the shop through her eagerness to have done with the place. Ross was still there, standing talking to Miss Ward and a lady from one of the shore bungalows. All three looked round as the bell alerted them to Zoë's appearance.

'Oh—did you want the shop? I was just about to close,' she asked the newcomer.

'Thank you, but no,' the woman replied. 'We were just having a wee gossip.'

Hoping she had not been the subject of it, Zoë turned

away with a smile and began to wrestle with the intricacies of the sunblind mechanism. She heard Ross's voice.

'Actually, Miss Ward, I was on my way up to Innistulach to check the deer fence. Alec Bayne phoned today to tell me that one of the posts is rotten and giving way. I rather wanted to cast an eye over your place and the others too. If you came up in the Range Rover with me you could put me in the picture about anything that needs doing and save me a bit of time.'

'Well—if it saves you, Mr Macallister,' Zoë heard Miss Ward say. She cast a surreptitious glance over her shoulder and met Ross's eyes as he took the old lady's bag and slipped a hand under her arm to escort her over the road.

'Goodnight again, Zoë,' he called, no doubt to underline the final lesson in people-handling for the day.

She called a falsely bright goodnight and took out her temper on the sunblind, which retaliated by folding into its metal casing with vicious suddenness trapping her finger so hard that Zoë couldn't smother an agonised yelp.

Ross, who had just settled Miss Ward in the passenger seat of the Range Rover, strode quickly back across the road.

'Hurt yourself?'

'No. It's nothing.' But her finger refused to back her up and promptly proceeded to gush blood. She made to put it in her mouth but Ross caught her hand.

'Don't do that. You're not a vampire. Let me see.' He inspected the cut. 'You'll need to disinfect this.'

Zoë wanted to get her hand away from his disturbing touch. 'I'll do something about it later.' She pulled a clean handkerchief out of her pocket and wrapped it round the finger.

'You'll do something about it now.' He turned and

called across to Miss Ward, 'I'll just be a moment, Miss Ward,' then propelled Zoë firmly indoors. 'Come on. I know where Fiona keeps the first-aid kit, and I don't suppose you do.'

'You seem to know everything,' Zoë said ungraciously, following him resignedly through to the back of the shop.

He dealt with her finger briefly but thoroughly. 'That blind had rust on its metal. Have you had a tetanus jab recently?'

'Last summer. So you see I'm prepared for all eventualities.'

Though not for the memories that his touch brought crowding back. How strange that they should still be there beneath all the layers of experience laid down in the intervening five years. But then, everything was, wasn't it? All the hurt, all the pain, and all the pleasurable experiences, just waiting for the right trigger to bring them up to the surface.

'All right?' He was looking at her, reading heaven knew what in her eyes.

'Fine, thanks. You really needn't have bothered.'

'I'll put a drop of oil on the hinges of that blind as I go out, then it shouldn't happen again.' He gave a sudden, unexpected, slight grin. 'Yes—I know where Fiona keeps the oil too! Goodnight, Zoë.'

She stayed in the back of the shop until she heard him drive off, then, deciding that she really couldn't face seeing him yet again up at Innistulach—because he would surely come over to Morag's cottage too to check whatever he had mentioned checking over the phone— Zoë decided on a prudent walk along the shore until she saw the Range Rover come down the track again. Enough was enough for one day.

She walked well beyond the end of Innistraigh with

many pauses. The cormorants were perched on the rocks, hanging out their wings to dry in characteristic pose. There were shellduck and merganser, some with flotillas of ducklings bobbing along behind them like bathtub toys. These called for an extra-long halt. When she had retraced her steps almost to where the car was parked, walking on the crunchy stones of the beach, she saw an oystercatcher trailing a wing and realised that it was attempting to decoy her away from its eggs which would be well camouflaged amongst the pebbles but incredibly at risk.

So careful was she being where she put each foot that Zoë didn't see Ross's Range Rover until it was almost down on the road. She had meant to be driving along, passing him within the safe shell of her car. Instinctively she flung herself towards the sea wall and crouched down against it, holding her breath and praying that he would go straight past.

The gods were not listening. He swerved on to the verge and jumped out to stand looking down at her ridiculous position before she could even let out the breath she was holding.

'Now what have you done?'

She scrambled to her feet, trying to look self-possessed. 'Nothing. Why?'

'You fell. Lurched towards the wall like a sack of potatoes. Done any damage?'

'No! I said I hadn't.' Her voice strengthened. 'Ross— I don't need a minder. I'm quite capable of looking after myself.'

'I'd question that on this afternoon's record. Are you sure you're all right?'

'*Yes*. As a matter of fact——' her brain was beginning to function again '—I was following an oystercatcher trailing its wing. I thought I might see the young ones.'

'Not if you were following the adult. The nest is nowhere near the wall, anyway. It's over by that big rock.'

'Trust you to know that too.'

'So it's a good job that I stopped after all, don't you think? Now you can see the chicks. Don't go near the nest though, will you?'

'I'm not a savage.'

'Just a bird-lover's cautionary warning. Well—I hope you manage the rest of the way back to the cottage without further incident.' Amusement flickered at the back of his eyes.

'Oh—why don't you go home?' Zoë said, and crunched off to her car.

As she drove up the track, she marvelled that she, who held down responsible jobs and looked after herself very well, thank you, could turn into the sort of idiot she seemed to be becoming here. As she remembered Ross's tongue-in-cheek remark about a touch of sophistication, the humour of the last little escapade struck her, and the laughter that convulsed her made her feel better.

Polly's welcome was warm, no doubt more due to the delicious smell of beef casserole than to genuine affection. Zoë put on the vegetables and went upstairs to change into jeans and a favourite loose scarlet silk shirt. She had colour in her cheeks from her walk, banishing the London pallor, and her eyes looked bright, worthy of a bit of attention. By the time she had renewed mascara and eyeshadow and fluttered her lashes at Polly the vegetables were cooked and the two of them sat down to a highly satisfactory meal.

Zoë had washed up and made coffee when the knock came at the door. She expected Fiona, eager to show off her new hair-do, but it was—yet again—Ross who stood on her doorstep.

'I don't believe this!' The not very civil greeting was out before Zoë could stop herself.

'Sorry—but having checked two of the Innistulach properties I prefer to do this one so that I can cross them all off the list. It's tidier that way—and I did say I'd arrange something.'

'You could have come in earlier. Why didn't you get the key from Fiona?'

'I thought you might take a poor view of that, not being quite in harmony with our island ways.'

'When I'd suggested it?' She tried not to sigh. 'You'd better come in, then.' Zoë stood back, her dark head level with his shoulder as he passed her.

'It's a pleasant evening. I walked over the hill.' He sniffed. 'Coffee smells good.'

She couldn't very well not offer a cup after a blatant hint like that. 'Would you like some?'

'Love a cup.' He followed her into the kitchen, which suddenly seemed half its size and rather lacking in air. She hurried him through to the sitting-room where there was more space. They talked awkwardly like strangers until Polly came in and jumped up on to Ross's lap, kneading his thigh with her paws and purring loudly. 'She seems to have been well looked after. Fiona, I presume?'

'Yes—but she was back over here as soon as I turned up. Cats are very faithful to places, aren't they?'

'Like some people, I suppose?' He shot a penetrating look at her and she realised that once again the past was between them, certainly not intentionally recalled by her.

'Talking of places,' he went on quickly, perhaps regretting the revealing of his thoughts, 'I checked the outside of this one before I knocked. The tiles are fine but there's a bit of loose guttering at the back. I can get someone to see to that when the deer fence is being repaired. Any problems with windows?'

'I don't think so. I've had them all open.'

'Mind if I go round and check, just to make sure?'

'Help yourself.'

Zoë wondered if he had been feeling as scratchy and uncomfortable in her presence as she did in his. The conversation had creaked along like a rusty, unused gate. She just hoped he would go quickly. She even stood as she heard him coming downstairs but he went through to the kitchen and came back with his cup refilled.

'I helped myself,' he said, sitting down again. 'I want to have a talk with you about your future plans.'

'With regard to what?' she asked cautiously.

'The shop first. What are you doing about it? Sorry if I seem to be pushing you but it does concern me.'

Zoë swallowed her resentment that he was, whether she liked it or not, involved in her life. 'I'm trying to get someone to take it over and run it as Morag wished. I have an interview with Fiona's cousin tomorrow.'

'That sounds as though you intend to accept the legacy of the cottage. What are your plans for that?'

'*I* don't know! I only knew I was involved with the place at all yesterday. You might at least give me time to think.' Hostility crackled between them.

'If you do think. Once you leave here, if things follow the pattern of your last departure from Arran the island, everyone on it, and this cottage will be out of sight, out of mind. I don't want dead houses on my land, Zoë. I'd sooner buy it back from you.'

She got up and walked restlessly over to the window. 'If you feel like that, I'm surprised you didn't persuade Morag to make other arrangements in her will. I certainly would have done, if she'd given me any inkling of what she had in mind.'

'She knew that. That was why she never discussed it with you.'

'But since I am the one who is left with the cottage,' Zoë said firmly, moving back to her chair and perching on its arm, 'I must make it clear that however much you dislike the terms of the will, and however little you want to see me in possession of this place, it is nevertheless up to me to decide what I do with it.'

He returned her stubborn glare with level, unwavering grey eyes. 'If you think back to what I said, you will realise that I never implied that I didn't want you in the cottage. The reverse, rather. I don't want to see this place empty, left to rot. Don't forget you once made your opinion of this island abundantly clear to me.'

It was there again, the past that refused to be forgotten. Zoë had had enough of it. Suddenly it seemed glaringly obvious what she had to do. She must get rid of the guilt on her side, the resentment on his. She was sure that his attitude was fuelled by resentment.

She moved down into the seat of the chair, facing him. 'Ross, I think I owe you an explanation of why I behaved as I did that summer—to you and to everyone on Arran.'

Instantly his eyes were shuttered, impersonal, behind a barrier of male pride. 'Isn't that a bit unnecessary?' he said casually. 'What's the point of deliberately raking up the past?'

'We don't have to rake it up, do we? It's there every time we see each other, it seems to me,' she persisted, making herself keep on talking. 'I think we should have it out in the open and be rid of it once and for all, then perhaps we can start behaving like reasonable people.'

'I have never behaved unreasonably. And any such behaviour on your part was long enough ago for us to have forgotten it completely by now.'

'You told me that some things were never forgotten,

like remaining an islander no matter how long you were
away from the place. Remember?'

For a moment longer he looked at her with the eyes of
a stranger, then there was a detectable slackening of
tension and she knew that he was going to listen,
however reluctantly.

'Go ahead, then, if you must.'

She took an unsteady breath, trapping her hands
between her knees to stop them shaking because she was
very nervous. 'Nothing I did that summer was rational.
Let me begin at the beginning.'

Carefully she told him the manner of her father's death
and its effect on her.

'I really was not in my right mind that summer, Ross,'
she stressed. 'Everything I did was coloured by what had
happened. It made me hate Arran because my father's
suicide had brought me here. It made me suspect
everyone of having the potential to let me down—
because if you can't know what is going on in your own
father's mind while he plans his own death how can you
trust what anyone seems to be thinking? Then you came
back from London, and seemed to bring that old familiar
ground within reach again, to stop it shaking under my
feet. Well. . .' she looked up at him with a rueful half-
smile '. . .you know how I thought I felt about you. I
can see now that what I had done was to make you my
safe, older man to cling to—and I was all prepared to do
just that back in London until I learned that it wasn't
going to be like that. In my eyes—the eyes of a stressed,
possibly unbalanced teenager—you were another man
deliberately letting me down from choice. I'm sorry,
Ross. I don't presume to think that I hurt you, but I
must have puzzled you. And it was unbearably rude of
me not to answer any of those letters—which I am sure
were as kind as the whole of your behaviour to me that

summer. I hope you understand a little better now. For a while we were good friends. Can we at least not be enemies now?'

She held out her hand, inviting him to shake it. She had deliberately underplayed her own feelings for him that long-ago summer, and just as deliberately she had reduced his feelings for her to a sort of avuncular kindness.

He hesitated, but after a moment, with a slight shrug, his hand closed round her own.

'I'm not your enemy, Zoë,' he said simply. Relief went to her head and gave her the fleeting, wild desire to fling her arms round his neck. His next words proved how unwise that would have been. 'Thank you for telling me all that. I quite see that on this visit too you are probably emotionally unsettled by events. If having said all that makes you feel better, fair enough. I'm sure it will be better if we concentrate on business from now on, and save you further agonisings.'

In spite of their hands, still joined, she felt as though he had struck her. Was this his only reaction to all she had said? This blatant put-down?

'Perhaps you'll let me know as soon as you've made a decision about the cottage?' he went on, getting up and moving towards the door.

'I'll do that,' she said dispiritedly.

He was close to the little gate in the wicker fence when he turned round and made his only comment on what she had told him.

'You know. . .' There was an odd look in his eyes. 'I'd quarrel with you about one aspect of what you've told me.' His eyes scanned her face, then stared straight into her eyes as he said, 'I think there's a certain amount of self-delusion in your idea that you ever regarded me as a father-figure. If you're giving an explanation, let it be an honest one.'

Zoë felt a crimson tide wash up her face. 'It's no longer relevant, in any case,' she said. 'You have a wife, and I have Clive.'

'Clive? Ah—of course.' He waved his left hand derisively. 'The man who doesn't believe in signals.'

She looked at her watch. 'The man who has probably been waiting for me to phone him for the past hour. Forgive me if I don't stand at the door.'

'Of course,' he said, and with a brief nod closed the gate.

Zoë would have given anything for a long chat with Clive so that his wittily relayed London gossip could take away the heavy feeling she was left with after what had seemed to her such an emotional marathon. But the phone rang and rang in his apartment and remained unanswered. Clive was not available to work his urbane magic, and Ross's presence remained like a brooding, accusing ghost in the cottage.

CHAPTER THREE

IT WAS all arranged—at least, the 'who' was, if not precisely the 'when'. Catriona was the ideal person for Morag's shop. She was open-faced and pleasant, kind and sensible, and—above all—eager for the job.

Zoë, anxious to be fair, had asked her if she was absolutely sure that she wanted to uproot herself. Catriona's answer had left no doubts in the air.

'You're offering me a home in a place I love. You're giving me not just a job, but time for my daughter. And you're giving Isobel a little school by the sea instead of a shabby, overcrowded building in a city street. Can you really doubt that I want to accept your offer, Zoë? I don't just want it. I'm desperate for it. I've done nothing but think about it since Fiona phoned me yesterday.'

So it was settled. Zoë was even glad that the exact date of Catriona's availability was unsure because it further illustrated the sound quality of the girl. Although she did not at all care for her present job, she wouldn't leave it without working out sufficient notice to allow for her replacement to be found. She promised to phone Zoë with a firm date as soon as she had spoken to her employer.

It had been a highly satisfactory meeting, and on the strength of it Zoë treated herself to a salad and dawdled pleasantly over it, then wandered through the store's boutiques and treated herself further by succumbing to the temptation of a Jean Muir dress. It had the long, elegant, unfussy lines that suited her tall, slender figure, and its misty blend of blues echoed the changing colour of her eyes. Soon she would be wearing it in Cannes, she told herself, now that the problems Morag had wished on her were gradually being sorted out. Thoughts of Cannes prompted several more purchases, and she left the store well loaded with smart bags.

On the train, she brooded again a little about the unexpected terms of Morag's will. Involving someone who had made it so clear she had no fondness for Arran seemed unwise to say the least of it, and Morag had never lacked wisdom. In a way, though, Zoë reflected, she was glad of the problems. Dealing with them went some small way towards making up for her neglect of Morag. It was a form of atonement.

Bad timing meant that it was the six o'clock boat she caught back to the island, the last one of the day, but it was a lovely evening and the cries of the gulls following the boat were so much more pleasant than the roar of Glasgow's traffic.

Alec Bayne had given her a lift into Brodick that morning, so she was coming down the ferry's gangplank resigned to having to phone for a taxi when she heard her name called, and looked across the road to see the now familiar sight of Ross and his Range Rover, the back of which was loaded with boxes.

'Want a lift?' he called.

Zoë decided that it would be silly to stand on her dignity and refuse, and went over to join him.

'I seem to be seeing rather a lot of you,' she said as he took her parcels and made room for them in the back with his load.

'Someone who claims to want friendship shouldn't complain about that,' he said rather surprisingly. 'But this is pure coincidence, I assure you. I've been picking this lot up. It came over on the last ferry, but I've only just got round to it.'

She settled herself beside him and they were quiet
while he negotiated the temporary crowds leaving the
ferry.

'So—how did it go with Fiona's cousin?' he asked.

'Fine. She's willing, and very suitable. Have you met
her?'

'Briefly. She seemed nice enough.'

Zoë told him about Catriona and Isobel, and found
that she was feeling more at ease with him now, as he,
apparently, was with her. So maybe yesterday had done
some good after all.

'Oh, look! The deer have come quite low down on the
hills,' she said as they drove along Shiskine. Ross slowed
down and halted, though he must have seen the sight
scores of times. They sat watching the leisurely movement of the russet pinpoints on the golden slopes, and
Zoë rested her head against the seat, drinking in the
quiet, sunlit peace.

'This is so lovely after Glasgow,' she said.

'Tell me about this Clive,' Ross said unexpectedly.
Instantly the easy calm was gone, and Zoë instinctively
sat up straight in her seat.

'There's not a lot to tell. Look at the time. Aren't you
expected back at Innis Howe?'

His jaw had that stubborn look, and she could tell he
was going to persist. 'You can leave me to judge that. Is
he a Londoner?'

'Yes. At least, I think so.'

'Only think? Where does his family live?'

'He hasn't really mentioned them. I don't know if he
has any.'

'You don't know much, do you? Still, families can
create complications, can't they? No family, no strings
to pull in the wrong direction.'

She shot a glance at him and he smiled disarmingly—the smile on the face of the tiger, she felt.

'Do you work with him?' he went on.

'For him,' she answered shortly. 'He's partner in the wine-importing firm I'm with now.'

'And quite a catch, is he?'

'I'm not trying to "catch" anyone. We get on well. We both love London, like the theatre, laugh at the same things.'

'Sounds very jolly. Oh—and you both think rings are not necessary.'

'Ross!' she said emphatically, stung into attack. 'You're being nosy, and not very nice. Could we get on?'

'Just interested,' he said. 'I'm sorry. I didn't realise it was a bit of a sore subject.'

'Who said it was?' Zoë answered too quickly. 'Clive and I are good friends.'

'Well, that seems very. . .satisfactory, then,' he said, adding with solemn wickedness, 'Friendship is a highly valuable thing.'

He still seemed reluctant to get going again, and Zoë sensed that he was looking not at the view but at her. Eventually his voice broke the—for her—uncomfortable tension that seemed to be growing between them.

'What you told me last night was something of a shock. I think my reaction to it was perhaps a little more brusque than it should have been.'

An apology? As near as he would come to it, anyway.

'There wasn't really much to be said after all this time, was there?' she told him prudently, letting him off lightly.

'You were so young and vulnerable. I was always conscious of that. But if I had known the deeper hurt behind the one I was aware of I should have treated you even more like fragile china.'

Zoë felt a dangerous responding warmth well up in her at his words, and masked it with flippancy. 'Don't worry! There were no breakages!'

'I attributed your behaviour to your years,' he went on, still serious. 'If I had realised what truly caused it, I might have reacted in a much more emphatic way to your flight from Arran.'

And if he had. . . If he had come after her instead of sending a few unopened letters? Zoë dragged herself back from a mythical present with herself as Ross's wife.

'I had a lot of growing-up to do,' she said briefly, 'and now I've done it.'

'I don't feel one hundred per cent sure of that.' Ross's words made her turn her head and look at him. 'You're still into hasty decisions,' he went on, grey eyes daring her to look away. 'Look at that business with the cottage and shop. Bearing in mind that you are a person who lives an impossible distance away, is incredibly busy, and hates Arran—taking all that on hardly seems to spring from the wisdom of age.'

'Call it whatever you like—I'm determined to do it for Morag's sake.' Zoë's blue eyes stared with defiant determination into his. 'You pointed out that I had a fair amount of neglect to make up for and I freely admit that. Well, now I'm doing the making-up. And don't say it's too late to do anything for Morag. Anything I do for the community at Innistraigh is for her, and I know she would be glad.'

'Fair enough.' He went on looking at her. 'But does this Clive person come into the "wise decisions" category? Or is he just in your emotional life because he happens to be around and you're thinking it's about time you'd made some progress in that direction?'

'Ross!' Her cheeks flamed. 'You go too far. Leave my personal life to me. Now—please can we go?'

'Hmm. . .' He went on holding her with his eyes for a sceptical moment, his expression conveying that he knew he was right. When didn't he? Zoë thought furiously, remaining obstinately silent.

'Very well, then. Off we go.' He started up the engine and pulled on to the road again.

Zoë went on silently thinking about Clive, and not enjoying her thoughts. The trouble with being questioned about Clive by Ross was that Ross's personality and physical stature—not to mention the fact of his actual presence beside her in the Range Rover—tended to make Clive seem just a bit. . . She sought an appropriate word, came up with 'insubstantial' and didn't like it. It made her feel disloyal, and she began to review all the things she enjoyed about Clive. There was his wittiness—though that could be a little cruel sometimes. He took her to clubs and shows and restaurants that she would certainly not see the inside of without him. . .though she never seemed to get round to visiting the outdoor hidden corners of London that she so loved these days. Clive found them dull. She decided that she was getting nowhere with her thoughts, and that it was Ross's fault. He had started up this chain of questions, and look at him. He was driving along, gently whistling to himself, as though he had never stirred up the hornet's nest in her mind. She wanted to be away from him—now.

'Just drop me at the foot of the track,' she told him as they neared the turn-off for Innistulach.

'I'll drive you up.'

'No—really. I want to call in on someone.' Now he had got her lying to avoid the necessity of inviting him in for a 'thank-you' drink and thus prolonging the time with him.

It was a relief when he didn't persist, and she could

watch the Range Rover disappear from sight before setting off up the track to the cottage.

She was still lost in thought as she deposited her bags on the floor in the hall, and it was only when the rustle and crackle of paper stopped that she realised the noise had masked another—the careful but still audible sound of someone treading warily down the stairs.

The carpenter's warning, which she had not taken too seriously, came back to her instantly. She stood, momentarily paralysed, watching the shadow that was now appearing and growing on the paved floor of the hall, too terrified even to cry out for Fiona or Alec.

The toe of a well-polished shoe appeared on the bottom step, then charcoal trousers, Italian jumper—a familiar one—and, finally, a smugly smiling face.

'Surprise, surprise!' Clive said, stepping down into the hall. 'I hoped it might be you. Where on earth have you been all day?'

Zoë leaned, trembling with reaction, against the wall. 'Clive! You scared the living daylights out of me. What in the world are you doing here?'

He pushed back fair hair that flopped forward in a way that had always reminded Zoë of a younger Michael Heseltine. Why did it suddenly seem a little effete?

'Coming to sort you out, sweetie. I thought it was rather necessary. And I expect a warmer welcome than that!'

He opened his arms in mock pleading, and she moved into them, relieved. . .but rather because he was not the intruder she had suspected than because he was here, she realised in a corner of her mind.

He ran his hands proprietorially down the curve of her back. 'That's more like it.'

'I phoned you last night—or tried to,' Zoë said.

'I was on my way. Had the worst night of my life just

before Carlisle in a mausoleum of solid granite with a
bed to match. You owe me for that.'

'Poor you. What time did you get here?'

'Early afternoon. I'd seen all there was to see three
times over within half an hour. I've been incredibly
bored. All this empty space—and cows that look as
though they've rugs on their heads. Weird!'

Zoë laughed, warming to him. 'You were never meant
for the rural scene, Clive.'

'Amen to that.' He held her at arm's length, growing
serious. 'And neither were you. Hence my presence to
remind you of that fact.'

'I know.' She moved away and pulled the blue dress
out of one of her bags. 'I *am* planning ahead. I bought
this for Cannes today. What do you think? She held it
against herself and did a little twirl.

'Oh—so we really are going to get there eventually?'
He was not going to be distracted. There was that steely
look in his eyes behind the masking smile that she had
seen in the course of so many business deals. 'Two more
days, Zoë. And not a second longer. That's the dead-
line—and I mean it.'

'I'm almost there. While I feed you—you must be
hungry—I'll tell you all I've managed to do so far.'

'Good.' He picked up a classy bottle of Grand Cru
Vaudésir '76. 'Here's a little something to have with
whatever you've got.'

She quickly upgraded the casserole. '*Boeuf bourguinon*,
and some rather good cheese I got in Glasgow. Help
yourself to whisky or whatever and I'll soon have it
ready.'

Zoë scooped up her shopping and took it upstairs,
feeling under pressure. The pressure increased when she
was confronted by Clive's suitcase in her room, his
dressing-gown on her bed alongside her own.

So that was the way he thought the wind blew, was it? Well, she had no intention of being orchestrated to that extent. Her mouth set determinedly as she went down and politely but firmly informed him that not only was he not sharing her room, but it would not be acceptable for him to stay in the cottage either. Morag would not have approved, and the elderly neighbour in the third Innistullach property would look askance. Zoë held out against his mocking disbelief until she thought she had convinced him.

Over dinner, she told Clive about Catriona, and as the wine flowed—more into Clive's glass than her own, she was careful to ensure—the meal progressed pleasantly.

But Clive had not been at all convinced of the need to move to a hotel, she found when she opened the telephone directory at the number of the Kinloch in Blackwaterfoot and offered to make a booking for him. 'There's a heated pool and squash courts,' she told him encouragingly. She didn't realise that Clive had left the table and come up behind her until she felt his arms slide round her, his hands crossing over her stomach, kneading her flesh and pulling her back against him.

'That's not the kind of activity I'm thinking of, my sweet,' he said in her ear, nuzzling her neck and kissing her. 'I thought by now you'd have forgotten all that nonsense. Come on. . .' The kisses intensified. 'Why don't we start our holiday right now? You know you want to as much as I do.'

Clive's lovemaking, as far as they had progressed, had always been persuasive, and he read too much into her initial surprised relaxing into his embrace. But Zoë was not going to be helped into bed by a little vintage wine— and certainly not here and now.

She pulled away determinedly, but his arms tightened like iron bands.

'Clive!' she said warningly. 'Let me go. Don't be crazy.'

'But I am crazy over you. You know that.' He seemed to have more than his fair share of hands and was managing to do far more than just hold her.

'I've warned you!' she panted, struggling harder than ever to free herself.

'I don't happen to want to listen to your warnings,' said the voice in her ear.

'All right!' She brought her heel back with vicious suddenness into his shin, and like magic she was free.

She watched with satisfaction Clive rub his leg as he staggered back into his chair. 'Don't say I didn't warn you. And don't think of starting all that again.' Her eyes were glittering with anger. She threw the telephone directory on to the table in front of him and slammed the phone down by the side of it. 'Take your pick of hotels and get booking. I'm going to leave you to it for a quarter of an hour. When I hear your car going, I'll come back down—and not before.'

'Cold, unfeeling bitch!' he muttered.

'You've still got another leg—so watch it!' she retorted, and left the cottage.

She felt angry enough to hand in her notice and send him packing, but no doubt both of them would regret an impetuous move like that once they calmed down. All the same, her progress up the hillside was fuelled by anger and she didn't think where she was going, only of the need to work off adrenalin in movement.

Her preoccupation, plus the gathering shadows on the hill, concealed the fact that someone was sitting in the place towards which she was mindlessly heading. She was almost falling over Ross before she knew he was there. It was embarrassing to realise that she had automatically made for their old meeting-place, which he obviously still considered his own.

'Oh——' She stopped. 'I never dreamed anyone would be up here. Didn't think where I was going, actually. Just stropped off up the hill.' That could have been more wisely put.

Ross moved up on the stone seat. 'There's room for two.' She hesitated, and he went on. 'Come on! At least give yourself the time to get your breath back. You came up the hill as though the hounds of hell were after you.'

She sat down, trapped between not wanting to stay but certainly not wanting to go back down yet. 'Watching me, were you? Well, I don't know about hounds. One hound, maybe.'

She sensed him smiling. 'Come, come, Zoë. That's no way to speak about a man who's come all this way to see you.'

She rounded on him, exasperated that he apparently knew all about Clive's arrival. She was surrounded by men trying to force her into one course of action after another. 'What goes *on* in this place? Can't anybody do anything without the word being passed round? Go on— tell me what time he left London. I'm sure you know. I bet you even know the colour of his underwear. Really!'

'I wouldn't dream of enquiring into such personal matters,' Ross said unflappably. 'Can I help it if the famous Clive asked one of my men the way to Morag's? He must be a very caring friend indeed to follow you all this way, Zoë.'

'It's like having the secret police snooping around.' She glowered out at the Sound. A car engine started up below them. Zoë listened to it, following the headlamps' progress down the track. 'Well—you might as well pass this around to the network that briefs you. I'm sure they're interested. Clive is now on his way to the Kinloch, where he will spend the night.'

'With your blessing? No, probably not,' he said,

studying the tetchy look she was giving him. 'Those eyes of yours always did change colour when you lost your temper, and there's just enough light to see that they've done it now. What happened to spoil the reunion? Come on—get it off your chest, girl. You'll feel better afterwards.'

'That's my business, and I have no intention of letting the whole of Arran know it.'

'I can make a pretty informed guess. Our friend thought he'd get a warmer welcome—and maybe a warmer bed, did he?'

She remained stubbornly silent, eventually saying, 'I'm not talking about it, Ross. It's no concern of yours.'

'And yet only twenty-four hours ago you were so desperately eager to talk.'

'On a matter that did concern you. This doesn't.' She pointedly changed the subject. 'The Sound looks lovely tonight.'

He stood with determination. 'If you're unwilling to have a real conversation, I'm certainly not indulging in mindless social chit-chat.'

Zoë sighed and got up to face him. 'Ross, as you reminded me, I made a big attempt at communication yesterday. It didn't seem to remove whatever causes us to argue every time we meet.' Still he was silent. 'Well— it's true, isn't it?' she persisted. 'I told you honestly why I behaved as I did. . .' Honestly? The question flashed into her mind, unbidden, at the memory of her deliberate distortion of the emotions of five years ago. 'And where did that get me?'

'You gave me *a version* of why you behaved as you did,' he corrected.

'What do you mean by that?'

'I mean that on further consideration I'm not sure that I accept it as the real explanation.'

She turned away from him in annoyance. 'You seem to have something different to say on that score each time the subject comes up. In any case, that's your problem. If you don't want to believe me I can't make you do so.'

'I find it easier to believe something far more simple and prosaic,' he said.

'I'm not going to ask you what that is, if that's what you're waiting for,' she said after a little silence. She began to get up but a hand on her shoulder eased her gently but determinedly back into the rocky seat again.

'I think. . .that once you knew I was tied to Innis Howe, you remembered the state of the place—how run down and shabby it was—after which you started doing sums and didn't like the answers you came up with. I think it was probably as simple as that. You were a fairly privileged young lady, and you didn't fancy lowering your standard of living.'

It was such an unexpectedly offensive suggestion that Zoë found herself struggling with an overwhelming, humiliating desire to cry.

'You're not going to deny that, then?' He was looking extremely searchingly at her, and still she couldn't speak. 'Too close to the mark, am I? Sometimes silence communicates a whole lot more than words, Zoë.'

She swallowed hard. 'What's happened to make you like this, Ross? You never used to enjoy being cruel. How can you make such an unpleasant, unfounded accusation?'

'Can you deny that the day you came to Innis Howe with the others was something of an eye-opener?'

She remembered the depressing effect his home had had on her, at a time when depression was never too far away. Surrounded by trees, their branches pressing against the windows, and the shabby interior with carpets so worn that it was hard to distinguish any colour in them, the whole place had cried out for time and money to be spent on it. She had certainly been shocked by it. That Ross should come from such a dreary, spartan background seemed all wrong. Ross to her meant warmth, caring, and light in dark places. His home spoke only of cold neglect and darkness. Yes, she had been shocked, but not in the way he implied.

'I'm not denying that,' she said reluctantly.

'I thought as much.'

'But neither do I accept that money came into it.'

He removed his hand from her shoulder. 'Nevertheless, once you knew that Innis Howe was part of the package deal your interest in me soon waned. It took no more than a few seconds for the ardour to evaporate, as I recall. Are you going to deny that?'

She shifted impatiently on the stone seat. 'Oh—what's the point of going on about the past? I've given my explanation.'

'You were the one who thought the subject needed resurrecting.'

That was undeniable. 'Well, I was wrong,' she said flatly.

'All right. Let's talk about the present. Are you really going to marry this man?'

'Give him a chance to ask me!' The sudden change of subject shocked a less than wise answer out of her.

'If you were sure about him, you'd have your answer worked out in advance. Sending him off to Blackwaterfoot doesn't sound like a sign of enthusiasm to me.'

Indignation brought her to her feet again. 'Would you like a few intrusive questions on *your* private life, Ross? Shall I grill you on the subject of your own marriage since you seem so keen to pry into my hypothetical one? And, in any case, how come the upright Mr Macallister is implying that it's out of date to wait until marriage to spend the night with a man?'

'So he did try it on!' Ross said triumphantly.

'Mind your own damned business!' Zoë was nearing the end of her tether. 'What goes on in my private life is my private concern.'

'Even if it does have you running up here? You walked out on him at the cottage, didn't you? That was his car we saw leaving, well after you'd come up here.'

'Goodnight, Ross,' she said stonily.

He caught her sleeve and stopped her walking off down the hill. 'Just before you go, look what I found earlier.' He knelt down and pulled away the heather at the back of the stone seat—and there were the two bird carvings, partly covered with lichen, but their message winging straight across the years to drive out anger and replace it with the haunting memory of the girl she had been the day Ross carved them. She looked down on the slight silvering at his temple—indicative of who knew what had happened in the intervening years—and had a fierce longing to reach out and touch what was probably, she reasoned with herself, simply a sign of the passing of time.

'I haven't looked at them from that night to this,' he said softly, standing up after carefully pulling back the heather to hide the past. 'Strange to think that long after we've gone, they'll still be there, and no one will have the faintest idea why.'

They stood, silently looking at each other, caught by a memory that had frightening power.

'I don't somehow think that you were into the business of prudent waiting and seeing and sending would-be lovers packing that particular night, were you, Zoë?'

There was a huskiness in his voice that touched a responsive chord in her. She tried not to hear it.

'I've grown up since then,' she said, her eyes dropping from his. 'And you've married.' It was a pointed reminder to him—one that she thought he needed. And, judging by the sweating of her palms and the throbbing of the vein at her temple, one that she needed to give.

He stepped round in front of her and again barred her way. 'I don't want you to make a mistake, Zoë, that's all. I don't know why I sense that this business with Clive could be one, but I do. Perhaps it's the look in your eyes when you talk about the man. You don't look——' like she used to look when *he* looked at her. . .when they planned the future that was not to be together. Zoë knew that that was what he was thinking, but he completed the sentence impersonally and safely '—like a girl should when she is thinking of a man she loves.'

He was not touching her, and yet the way he was looking at her held her more than any physical grasp. It was as though, despite her resolve, he was challenging her to remember. . .and remember she did. The poignancy and the passion of the last time they were together in this place seemed to emanate from all around them, from the rock, the heather, the sky, and the dark, shining waters of the Sound.

But that time was past, and the memory of it must not be allowed to flare into impossible, dangerous life again. Zoë took a step backwards away from him, but fate was against her, making her stumble on the rough ground.

Then he actually did hold her, his hands gripping her upper arms to steady her initially, but she recovered her balance immediately, and still he didn't let go of her. He stared down into her face with such searching intensity

that fear fluttered in her throat—though of what she
didn't know.

'Life could have been very different for both of us,' he
said, and his eyes were disturbing.

'But it didn't work out that way.' She swallowed hard.
'And now we're firmly established with other partners.'
With an effort she looked away from that troubling,
burning gaze. Slowly he relaxed his grip on her arms and
let her go. What had happened? she asked herself. Apart
from a statement of obvious fact, absolutely nothing.

'It's getting dark,' she said with an attempt at normal
conversation. 'We'd better go home while we can still
see where we're going.'

'The voice of reason.' He laughed briefly, but without
much mirth. 'I expect you'll sort out your life to your
own advantage, Zoë. After all, that's been the order of
the day so far, hasn't it?'

'Goodnight, Ross.' She left him standing there, not
rising to the taunt, and walked back down the hill,
picking her way carefully in the gloaming. He was
wrong. Right now she felt that the least sensible thing
she had ever done was to walk away from him like this,
all those years ago.

There was nothing to be achieved by thinking on those
lines, though. The past could never be rewritten. You
made your choices, and you stood by them.

All the same, she wouldn't turn down the chance to
go back and be a less misguided, impetuous eighteen-
year-old if some fairy godmother should offer her the
chance. Ross was right. It could have been different for
both of them.

Back at the cottage she was relieved to confirm that
Clive had definitely gone. For all she knew, so locked
into the past with Ross had she been that Clive could
have come back for another wrestling bout.

How distasteful it seemed in retrospect, that undignified flurry of grabbing and kicking. Especially when thought about while her mind was full of Ross Macallister.

But she must remove him from the dangerous, dark places of her mind. Ross was another woman's husband, and not to be looked upon with the kind of feelings that had threatened her up on the hill.

It was strange that he had said so little—virtually nothing—about his wife. The explanation must be that each time the two of them met this charged, heavy atmosphere seemed to surround them, blotting out reality. It was crazy and it was wrong, and it must stop.

She tried hard to concentrate on her own circumstances and future. Her immediate project tomorrow would be to smooth Clive's ruffled feathers—which she was fairly confident of being able to do, since, for all his faults, he was no sulker. Then she must speed things up to the best of her ability so that they could get away from this place. It *had* been unwise to come back.

Yes. . .her own future. That was what she must concentrate on.

But her own future, try though she might to plan it, remained a cloudy uncertainty, while, compelling as magnetic force, two long-ago carved birds circled and hovered in her mind.

CHAPTER FOUR

CLIVE phoned early next morning, cool at first, but thawing rapidly and his tone becoming much more conciliatory when he realised that Zoë wasn't in the least repentant. He seemed to have expectations of being amused throughout the day, but Zoë soon disillusioned him. She had loads to do and she wished very much that he had not embarked on this chase after her. He was only complicating matters.

She reminded herself, though, that she had upset his business plans, possibly curtailed their holiday, and that he was her boss after all. Last night's little episode would have meant the end of any relationship, business or otherwise, for some men. She supposed that Clive was, in his own way, being fairly reasonable—today, at least.

'Do you think you can occupy yourself until sixish?' she said. 'I'll be through by then, with everything arranged.' She crossed her fingers behind her back as she said this.

'It had better be,' Clive sighed. 'What on earth am I to do with myself? Count seagulls?'

Zoë listed one or two places to visit. 'Then you can pick me up at the shop and we'll go and eat somewhere.'

'Scared to have me at the cottage again?' She could imagine his jaundiced look. 'You needn't be. I've a healthy respect for your right foot after last night.'

She didn't rise to that, merely explained that she couldn't work all day at the flat and shop, make a hundred and one arrangements, *and* cook a meal.

'Fair enough, I suppose,' Clive said grudgingly. 'Thank heaven it's only for another twenty-four hours.'

She had had her bath and was halfway through dressing when the phone rang again. Assuming that Clive wanted to have a further moan, Zoë picked up the handset and said half jokingly, half in irritation, 'Now what?'

'That's a rather strange greeting,' Ross's voice said.

Zoë held the phone away from her as though it were about to bite, and stared at it before bringing it slowly back to her ear and saying cautiously, 'I thought it was someone else.'

'Has he phoned you already? You must have him worried.' When she didn't take him up on that he went on, 'How are you this morning?'

'I'm very well—and I trust you are. But I hardly think you rang me up to enquire about my welfare. Did you have some other purpose?' she asked sweetly.

'I did, of course. Is this a convenient moment? You've not just jumped out of the bath?'

Zoë shrank into herself as though he could see her bare limbs and lacy scraps of underwear. She reached out for her kimono and shrugged into it while she said, 'This is as convenient as any time will be today. But I've a lot to do, Ross. I'd be glad if you'd come to the point.'

'Right away. Something occurred to me about this situation between you and Clive.'

'Ross!' she protested sharply. 'It really isn't a matter about which you should concern yourself.'

'Why not? You're a member of the human race. Why shouldn't I feel neighbourly concern?'

She slumped back against the pillows. 'And that pretentious sort of twaddle doesn't fool me. You have an exaggerated interference factor in your make-up. But go on. I expect I'm going to have to hear the great thought.'

'Very well. It's this. I think the fact that you work for this Clive puts you into a vulnerable position when it comes to personal relationships. I'm serious about this. It's bound to influence how you behave towards him. Everything will be coloured by the fact that he's your boss. You're more flattered by his attentions than you ought to be *because he's your boss*. You go along with his wishes against your own, maybe, *because he's your boss*. Do I make myself clear?'

'As crystal. Do go on,' Zoë said with dangerous quietness.

'So the remedy's obvious. You need to change your job. Once you've done that you'll be able to assess honestly what you feel about the man, instead of being pressurised into something that's probably quite wrong for you.'

'You insufferable big-head!' she exploded. 'Not satisfied with overseeing the terms of Morag's will and then trying to interfere in my personal life, you now want to reshape my career. Being seigneur of your little kingdom seems to have gone to your head, Ross.' She paused to draw breath and went on with emphatic slowness, 'I really do not need all this advice.'

'Think about it. That's all I'm asking,' he said, undeterred. 'A man in a position of authority can be dangerous if he's involved in your emotions.'

'Any man throwing his weight around can be a pain in the neck,' she said pointedly. 'And, in any case, aren't you rather forgetting that I didn't exactly allow myself to be influenced by Clive's so-called position of authority last night?'

'But I don't know what happened last night, do I?' he asked smoothly. 'You were very careful not to tell me about it.'

'Nor do you know Clive, or you wouldn't be talking all this nonsense about him being dangerous.'

'It has occurred to me that it might be interesting to remedy that.'

Zoë thought of Ross and Clive together, and suppressed a shudder.

'I think not,' she said emphatically. 'Enough of all this, Ross. I have plans to make and things to do if Clive and I are to leave Arran tomorrow—which we fully intend doing.'

'You do? Then at least let me ask you to think seriously and calmly about the job situation.'

'I am calm. And I have thought. The subject's closed. Goodbye, Ross.'

'For now,' he said ominously.

Zoë put the phone down hoping that that was the last of it. She had seen and heard too much of Ross. He unsettled her—and he was not getting to work on Clive with those critical powers of his if she could help it.

It was a day of mixed success. The flat was prepared for Catriona, who phoned to say that she would be able to leave Glasgow in three weeks' time. Fiona thought she would be able to arrange a delayed start for herself at the Bell Rock, but couldn't track down the receptionist to sort this out definitely. The shelving suppliers promised the shelving 'within the next two weeks' but refused to be precise about a date. Zoë disliked leaving everything up in the air, but she was determined now to go. Apart from her job commitment, she was definitely feeling that she had to get away from Ross. Things would probably sort themselves out during her two weeks abroad, and if not she would face that situation when she came back.

* * *

'How was your day?' she asked Clive when she ran out to meet him at the end of the afternoon.

'Bleak. Empty roads and hillsides. Waves breaking on the shore. One wave's very like another, you know. I could almost hear time creaking by.' His face became more animated. 'Things looked up a bit late this afternoon. I was having a drink to bring me back to life, and actually met someone it was enjoyable to talk with.'

'You city snob!'

'Not really. It's a matter of finding common interests. As far as those go, you've got to agree that I'm a pretty exotic bird in these surroundings. The kind the natives peck to death.'

She looked at his upper-crust, public-school profile, his man-about-town clothes, and didn't deny it. 'I suppose you are. So who was this rarity who managed to get on your wavelength?'

'Someone who'd actually lived in London. For several years, in fact.'

It was not beyond possibility that other residents on Arran had done as much, but Zoë immediately felt a stab of unease. Clive's next words justified her suspicions.

'He knows you slightly,' he said. Macallister. Big fellow. Does the name ring a bell?'

More of a carillon, actually, Zoë thought weakly. 'Yes, I've met him,' she said warily.

'I can't think why he wants to bury himself up here. He seemed pretty well versed in what was going on in the City. Still he passed a pleasant enough hour for me.'

'Where did you meet?'

'At the Kinloch. He happened to come in and saw me at a loose end. Asked if I was on holiday. Then when I mentioned your name, we really started talking.'

I bet you did! Zoë thought explosively. And she was the fool who had mentioned the name of Clive's hotel to

Ross. What on earth did he think he was doing? How dared he actually set about vetting Clive's suitability? *Happened* to come in! That was a laugh—if anything in the situation called for laughter.

'One more thing,' Clive was continuing. 'We've no problem about where to eat tonight. Macallister's invited us round to his place for a meal. How about that? He's quite a landowner, I was told.'

There were several reasons she could give him to account for her horror at the thought of Ross and Clive at the same table, but none that she actually wanted to give him.

'You would be very disappointed, Clive. I went there once when I was last staying here. It's a pretty dismal place. Very neglected, and quite depressingly shabby,' she said as discouragingly as possible.

That didn't put him off in the least. 'It didn't sound so to me,' he said. 'And in any case I've committed us to going. Seven o'clock, he said. So there's time for a drink somewhere first if you need cheering up.'

She refused to fall into Ross's trap as easily as that. Apart from the Clive business, it had occurred to Zoë just how embarrassing she would find it to be the former girlfriend sitting at table with the present wife. Surely neither of them would find that particularly desirable. She pretended to be searching for something in her bag.

'Wait a minute, Clive. I seem to have left my cottage key in the shop. I'll go and get it.'

Fiona was just leaving, and as soon as she was out of the way Zoë picked up the phone and dialled the Innis Howe number. Ross answered. She had not considered the possibility of his wife's doing so.

'Ross—what are you playing at?' she fired at him.

'Playing at? What do you mean?' His voice was pure innocence.

'You know perfectly well what I mean.'

'I'm not exactly playing at anything. As a matter of fact I've just had a shower and now I'm about to get into something to grace the social scene this ev——'

'Ross!' she interjected. 'I've no time for fooling. How can we go through this farce of a meal tonight with you vetting Clive like someone from MI6 and scowling your disapproval at me behind Clive's back?'

'So I'm going to disapprove, am I?' he asked with interest.

'You know perfectly well you are. You're determined to do so.'

'So much perfect knowledge attributed to me in the course of one short conversation! I'm flattered.'

She swallowed her fury and tried to negotiate. 'Look— this isn't going to be enjoyable for any of us.'

'Then you only have to refuse to come.'

She bit her lip for a second. 'I can hardly do that, can I?'

'Why not?'

'Because then Clive would want to know why—and I'd have to tell him.'

'I see. Yes. I can quite understand the problem. He wouldn't enjoy the explanation, would he? So there doesn't seem much we can do about it, does there?'

'Yes, there is. You can ring me at the cottage in a few minutes and give some reason for cancelling—another engagement your wife has reminded you about, for instance.'

'Oh. . . I don't think I could do that,' he said with false regret.

'Why not?'

'It wouldn't be true, would it?'

'I hate you for this, Ross!' she said passionately.

'Do you?' The question hung in the air. 'I'm not going

to do anything to embarrass you tonight,' he said after a fuming, frustrated silence from her. 'What do you imagine I'll do? Try to make a fool of your precious Clive? Does one really have to try to do that? He struck me as being capable of doing it himself, without assistance.'

'You are unbearably rude,' Zoë told him icily.

'Just a truthful, impartial observer. Of course, I know you're biased. And therein lies the danger. . .'

'*Why* did you have to do this?'

'You know why. I haven't made any secret of it. So you're going to have to opt out of this evening honestly, Zoë, or else grin and bear it.'

She slammed the phone down. She was only banging her head against a granite wall by arguing.

Upstairs at the cottage she surveyed her rather scant range of clothes. She was going to have to wear her new dress. Nothing else she had brought to Arran was really suitable for a dinner party—and one for which she needed to boost her self-confidence to such an extent. She grimaced as she took it off its hanger. This was not the kind of occasion she had meant to christen it with, but, if it got her through the evening, well and good.

She pinned her hair into the sort of sophisticated top-knot the Jean Muir seemed to call for and put on a pair of large pendant turquoise and silver earrings that were just right. Clive's head-to-toe look gave her the seal of approval.

'Beautiful, Zoë. Dangerously so, in fact. Good job we're going out. You're worth a ten-star meal from Macallister.'

Zoë would rather have eaten ashes elsewhere than the most sumptuous meal at Ross's table, but this thought, like many others, she kept to herself. She felt that she was beginning to understand the force that built up in a volcano prior to eruption. Only she couldn't afford to explode.

The minute they entered the Macallister estate Zoë began to suspect that Ross had a further motive for inviting them this evening. He had accused her of rejecting the lower standard of living she thought he would offer her on Arran. Now he intended her to see what she had turned down.

Things had changed vastly since she was last here. The estate was so well maintained now that she hardly recognised it. They passed a sign announcing the entrance to the Glen Innis Trekking Centre, and horses raced away from the car as it disturbed the peace. On the opposite side of the drive among the trees Zoë could see Swiss-type log chalets, well spaced, obviously holiday-letting accommodation of the most highly desirable standard.

Innis Howe itself, when they reached the house, was freed from its once oppressive barrier of trees and catching the evening sun so that its stone warmed to subtle ochre and its windows shone in welcome. The grounds, wide open now and glowing with colour, were attractively landscaped, taking advantage of the natural contours of the Glen.

'Not much sign of deprivation that I can detect,' Clive said.

She had no time to answer. Ross was coming out to greet them from the open doorway, elegantly casual in light grey trousers, fine white cashmere sweater and tweed jacket. Very solid, very real, very much the genial host.

'Good to see you both,' he said, shaking hands with the two of them. Seeing Ross beside Clive, Zoë could understand Clive's description of him as a 'big fellow'.

'What an amazing chance meeting that was, don't you think, Zoë?' he went on.

'An utterly unbelievable one,' she said, her back to Clive and the dirtiest of looks directed towards Ross though she took care to speak in the most pleasant of tones.

'You're looking very lovely tonight,' he told her smoothly, smiling innocently into her thunderous face. 'As radiant as the evening.'

'Attractive place you've got here,' Clive said, looking round.

'We've done a fair bit of work on it over the past five years.'

'It certainly took Zoë's breath away. She'd led me to expect something more Dickensian.'

Zoë could have gagged Clive with pleasure, but decided to try to play it straight. She slipped a hand through Clive's arm as they walked to the house.

'You must be very proud of what you've achieved, Ross. I congratulate you. I can understand your wanting to show it off.' It seemed impossible to speak without making a concealed dig at him, in spite of her intentions.

His grey eyes met hers as he stood back in the doorway. 'The place might have changed, but we're the same.'

'Speak for yourself,' she said lightly as she passed into the hall. 'I feel entirely different, thank goodness.'

Amber walls were reflected in a gleaming parquet floor on which rugs in glowing autumn colours made bright pools echoing the colours of the flowers in copper bowls on the side-tables. Shades of gold carried through into the sitting-room into which Ross led them, contrasting here with blues and bronze in the furnishing fabrics. The dark, mostly bad pictures of the older Macallisters' day had disappeared from the walls, giving way to modern oils and water-colours, the quality of which at once caught Clive's practised eye.

'Isn't that an Antonia Conti?' he said, going over to a bright oil of a girl in a market-place. 'Yes—I thought so.' He turned to Ross. 'A shrewd purchase. Her work is appreciating at a rate of knots.'

'Is it really?' Ross professed surprise. 'I suppose art is an investment to some people, but I'm afraid I just buy what I like.'

That's Clive marked down as mercenary, Zoë thought with resignation. Point one to the host in Ross's little game.

'You like the right things, then,' Clive said, refusing to be put down. 'Someone will be glad of it some day.'

'And good luck to them,' Ross smiled, dismissing the subject. 'Let me get you both a drink.'

As he took care of both of their requests, Zoë wondered uneasily when Ross's wife was going to put in an appearance. Since it had been arranged that they should meet tonight, she wanted to get on with it and not sit around nervously waiting for it to happen.

Ross seemed to read her mind. 'I'm afraid you're going to have to put up with a three-handed dinner tonight. My wife's away.'

Relief filled Zoë. 'That's a pity,' she said hypocritically. 'I was looking forward to meeting her.'

'So you don't know Mrs Macallister, then?' Clive asked, looking as though he suspected there might be more in this acquaintance than Zoë had admitted.

Ross answered him, but he looked at Zoë as he did so, making another of the double-edged statements that seemed to be featuring in the conversation. 'When your fiancée was last here the identity of the future Mrs Macallister was not quite settled, was it, Zoë?' He had deliberately recalled what had once been between the two of them, and he had used the word 'fiancée' with malice, Zoë knew. She felt her cheeks turn pink.

Ross purposely misread the signal. 'Is "fiancée" jumping the gun? If so, I apologise.'

Clive laid a casual arm round Zoë's shoulders. 'Zoë and I don't bother with categories, do we, sweetie? What's the point when we get on perfectly as we are? That's all that matters. But no doubt it's different in this part of the world.'

'A little,' Ross agreed pleasantly. 'We backwoodsmen are still rather prone to lay claim to our women.'

Zoë's eyes smouldered but she managed to sound merely amused. 'Don't put on the old-fashioned rustic act with me, Ross. It won't wash. You were well polished from years in the City when I first knew you, remember.'

'You two seem better acquainted than I thought,' Clive said, looking from one to the other with mischievous interest.

'Not really,' Ross said. 'I remember thinking when Zoë disappeared from Arran five years ago that in spite of several meetings I hardly knew her at all. However, here we are this evening—and with the added bonus of meeting you, Clive.' He stood. 'Perhaps if you're ready we should go through and eat.'

Clive gave her a speculative look as they went over to the dining-room. He was no fool, and he was picking up undercurrents that promised an even more interesting evening than he had expected. There was nothing he enjoyed more than delving into the hidden depths of the social scene. Zoë decided that she was going to have to try much harder if she wanted to avoid an embarrassing interrogation afterwards.

The dining-room walls were decorated with an impressionistic frieze of Arran landscapes.

'Here for you, Zoë, I think.' Ross pulled out her chair

and held it while she sat. 'You may find a view you recognise opposite you.'

He had seated her facing an unmistakable representation of the rocky seat high above Morag's. She deliberately looked to the right of where he was indicating.

'Oh, yes! The twelve Apostles at Catacol!' She pointed out the row of houses so named to Clive, and picked out other points of interest while Ross served the soup.

'That smells delicious,' she told him when he put a bowl in front of her. 'Don't tell me you made it?'

'No—I have an excellent housekeeper. Though I know you think I like to have a finger in every pie,' he added. Even if she tried to behave normally, Ross seemed bent on overloading every remark with significance.

Clive embarked on a series of anecdotes about meals he had eaten in various well-known London restaurants.

Ross listened with polite interest, and when Clive paused he said, 'Eating out seems to be one of your hobbies,' managing to make it clear to Zoë at least that he thought it was a pretty inane one.

'A necessity, not a hobby.' Clive explained the ways of the big city as though to a savage. 'It's the way to meet people. A lot of progress is made over a good meal.'

Ross glanced at Zoë. 'Of course. Even here. Though we are a little naïve most of the time. We simply enjoy sharing food with friends. But I do agree. There is the odd occasion when a position can be clarified over the table.' He refilled Clive's glass. 'Tell me, Clive. You're a man of business. What do you think are the chances of a small, independent general store in a place like this?'

Clive smiled knowingly. 'You mean like the one Zoë's lumbered with? No more chance than a snowflake in hell, if you ask me. I've told her I think she should offload it—but she's got this zany idea of keeping it going as long as possible.'

He went on at length in the same vein, damning himself with every word he uttered, while Ross sat back and listened patiently to a display of total indifference to community welfare.

'The chief obstacle to that, of course,' Ross said eventually, 'is the will itself.'

'You don't really take too much notice of that—not if you've got a lawyer worth his salt. A way can be found round most things by the right man. Why else would you pay him?'

Zoë had held her peace for long enough. 'Aren't you both forgetting something? The decision is mine to make, and I've made it. So let's change the subject.'

She felt ragged with the strain of knowing what was going on under the surface. Clive was being filleted like a kipper—all his weaknesses exposed. And because the idea of his having any weaknesses at all was totally alien to him he hadn't a clue what was going on.

She felt humiliated as the merciless manipulating of his unsuspecting victim by Ross went on throughout the meal. When they went back to the sitting-room for coffee, Clive slipped out to the car to collect his cigarettes and Zoë lost no time in turning on Ross.

'Satisfied?' she fired at him.

'Hardly the word I would have used. I'm more saddened to have my worst fears confirmed,' he said grimly.

'You're framing all your questions to get the answers you want from Clive,' she said heatedly.

'You know that he wouldn't produce the answers you've been listening to if they didn't spring straight from the sort of man he is.'

'You have a colossal cheek to inflict an evening like this on us!'

'Clive doesn't have the least idea that anything's being

inflicted on him,' Ross said grimly. 'And if anything should make you see sense that should. Oh—Zoë! If tonight makes you see things as they really are then I've done you a hell of a favour.'

'Some favour!' She was all set to say more, but Ross raised a warning hand.

'He's coming in. I know neither of us has said all we want to say, but it must wait.' He schooled his features into polite enquiry, and spoke to Clive. 'Ah—got them, have you? Good.'

Clive took his coffee and sat down unsuspectingly. 'Any chance of catching the financial news?' he asked, glancing at his watch. 'I've got some shares giving a little cause for concern.'

Another bad mark, Zoë thought hopelessly, seeing Clive through Ross's eyes as someone who couldn't forget finance for one short social evening. But Ross seemed delighted at the idea.

'Of course. As a matter of fact, I rather wanted to show Zoë the alterations we've made to the rest of the house. Perhaps now would be as good a time as any. You'll be happy with coffee and Armagnac and the radio?'

'Fine by me.' Clive was already pouring himself a generous glass from the bottle Ross had placed near him, and lost no time in turning up the volume on the radio, just as Ross lost no time in whisking Zoë out of the room.

Once in the hall he gripped her arm even more tightly and quickened his step with urgency that seemed to indicate that a casual tour of the house was the last thing he intended.

'Through here,' he said, sweeping her to the back of the hall and through a morning-room into the kitchen, where he closed the door firmly and turned on her.

'Are you really going back tomorrow?' he said, no longer the genial host.

'We are.'

'And you're not coming back?'

'Not unless it's absolutely necessary—for the shop, I mean.'

'Then, Zoë——' he gripped her shoulders and looked fiercely into her eyes '—that man is not for you. He's nothing more than a lightweight.'

She shook off his hands impatiently. 'How can you judge anything on an evening's acquaintance?'

'I tell you, there's no substance to him. Get deeply involved with him—if such a thing is possible—and you're going to be hurt.'

'What right have you to criticise my—friends?' she said. The hesitation had only been for a fraction of a second, but it was enough.

'You see?' He pounced on it at once. 'You don't even know what you can legitimately call the man. You deserve better than that, Zoë.'

Her heart was racing and her mouth dry with the panic his persistence was creating in her. 'How can you talk of what I deserve? You scarcely know me any better than you know Clive.'

'Oh—I know you.' The conviction is his deep voice was shattering. 'I knew you five years ago—and neither of us has forgotten a second of that time. No matter how long you disappear for, I shall know you whenever we meet. And I shall always be concerned about you.' He stepped closer, his eyes burning into hers. 'If you had come back here with a man who was half right for you, I would perhaps have held my peace. But a man like this one. . .' He seized her shoulders again. 'What must I do to convince you that I'm right? You need a real man of flesh and blood and guts—not that namby-pamby effete little bartender. Can't you see it?'

His face was contorted by the strength of his feelings, a strength Zoë couldn't understand. Why should he profess such persistent care about her, when only days ago he had scarcely been aware that she was still alive? It didn't make sense. But the force-field of his emotions was gripping her too so that the blood pounded through her veins.

'I could show you what it's like to be kissed by a real man, if you've forgotten,' he was saying. 'Would that make you see sense? If I made love to you, you wouldn't be undecided about the direction you want your life to take. You'd know. You'd have all the answers, and you wouldn't need a single question. You'd tremble for me as you're trembling now.'

It was true. She was only light seconds away from being swept along into his madness. But suddenly the explanation of his behaviour flashed into her mind, filling her with a sense of disappointment so vast that she felt to be falling through space. She tore herself away.

'I know what's wrong with you, Ross,' she said shakily. 'I've met men who behaved like this before, but I didn't expect it of you. You disappoint me.'

'What the hell are you talking about?' She could see the rapid rise and fall of his chest, but he didn't reach for her again.

'It's the old tacky story. Your wife's away, and you'll use any pretext to get someone to fill the gap. It's a common enough syndrome, the lonely husband. But I thought better of you—and you hid it under such a smokescreen of pseudo-care about me.'

She had succeeded in shocking him into control of himself. He looked at her grimly. 'Is that what you think?'

'What *else* can I think?' She wanted to convey how much she despised him for the way he had been behaving, but somehow her bitter disappointment that Ross—once her idol—should have proved to have feet of such common clay overwhelmed the scorn with which she had started to speak, and her voice broke.

'Don't you know me any better than that?' he asked, his voice tight with anger.

'You said earlier this evening that when I left Arran you felt you didn't know me at all. I'm beginning to think that you were a vastly fantasised figure to me.'

'Zoë——' He made the slightest of moves towards her, but at that moment there was a tap on the kitchen door. Ross swore and ran a hand through his hair. Zoë dashed a hand across her eyes and pretended to be looking out of the window.

'Yes?' Ross said tersely.

The door opened and a young girl stood there, smiling apologetically, holding a child of perhaps a year old in her arms. Zoë saw them reflected in the glass of the window, and the surprise of it made her forget her embarrassment and turn round. The child's face was streaked with tears and he was giving the uncontrollable reflex sobs that followed a bout of fierce crying. His fair hair and blue eyes had nothing of Ross in them, and yet as she saw the little boy's face light up at the sight of the man he saw, and Ross's grim face soften into loving concern, her surprise gave way to shock. She knew with stabbing certainty that this was Ross's son.

'I'm sorry, Mr Macallister,' the girl said, 'but Jonathan awoke in one of his states, and it seemed that nothing but a drink of juice and a look at you would settle him.'

'That's all right, Helen. You are doing exactly what I have told you to do. Come here, old chap.' He was taking the child from her with gentle hands, his tenderness banishing the remnants of Zoë's accusations. This was the Ross she had thought she knew—as caring and responsible in the field of fatherhood as he was in all others.

That at least was a consolation, but at the same time the situation seemed to be galloping sickeningly away from her. She had quite obviously shocked Ross with her accusation of a moment ago, but now he was the one at ease as he talked softly to his son, reassuring him. She, on the other hand, was finding herself simply devastated by the knowledge that he had a child. It mattered dreadfully to her.

It brought home to Zoë how much she had been relying on the fact that Ross's wife was insubstantial, unknown, miles away. But now awareness of all that a wife meant was there, physical and real, manifested in the soft, warm flesh of the child Ross was holding. He had loved this woman. He had made love to her, watched her grow big with his child. He had perhaps gripped her hands and wiped her forehead while the child was born.

It hurt. Beyond all reason and understanding, it hurt. She realised that what she was experiencing was plain, burning jealousy—and jealousy that she had not the least right in the world to feel. She, the level-headed manager of her own life, was suddenly at sea in it, pushed overboard by the sight of Ross and his child.

'You get the juice, Helen, and I'll dry these tears,' he was saying, walking through to the morning-room. Zoë, fighting to make sense of her feelings, followed him.

His eyes met hers over the baby's head, now tucked into the hollow of his neck for reassurance.

'I didn't know you had a son,' Zoë said with difficulty.

'And you thought I had forgotten?' His mouth twisted wryly, then softened as he ran a hand over the shining fair curls. 'You're wrong, Zoë. Jonathan is someone I never forget—not for a single moment of my life.'

'Why—why didn't you tell me about him?'

'When I was with you I was too involved in what was happening to you.'

She stretched out a hand and touched the starfish fingers, flesh of Ross's flesh. 'He's lovely. Not like you. . .'

'An unfortunate way to put it.'

She said in quick denial, because she had only been stating a physical truth, 'I wasn't trying to be rude.'

He relaxed again. 'I know you weren't. No—he's not like me. He's. . .himself. He has nightmares—at least, we think he does. He can't manage to tell us yet. All we can do is comfort him for whatever reason.'

The girl came back. 'Shall I take him now, Mr Macallister?'

'You'd better go ahead with the juice, Helen. I'll carry him back up to the nursery,' Ross said calmly.

Zoë had to get away. She was too unbalanced by this shattering development—shattering only because of its effect on her. She followed them out to the hall and called after Ross. He stopped and looked down at her, and the picture the two of them made twisted her heart again.

'I'll collect Clive and we'll go, then you needn't rush down,' she said.

He looked at her. 'Have we said all there is to say?'

She lowered her eyes. 'I just think it would be better if we left now.'

He didn't reply, and she ventured to look at him again.

'Why did you come back?' he asked bitterly.

'I'm asking myself that,' she said huskily.

'Zoë——'

'Goodbye, Ross.' She turned away and almost ran into the sitting-room.

Clive was himself. It surprised her. She felt as though the whole world and everything in it should have changed because her own feelings had suffered such an impact.

He switched off the radio. 'Did the nurse find you? She brought a wailing infant in here looking for Daddy.'

'Yes. Ross has gone upstairs with them. I said we'd be off.'

He stood and yawned. 'Might as well if the sprog's playing up. Oh, dear! The trials of domesticity. Doesn't exactly turn you on, does it? And Macallister doesn't look the type. Give me adult company any day. Unpredictable little beasts, children.'

She contrasted his careless, superficial words with the tender hands of Ross as he held his son, and for the umpteenth time that evening Clive came off worst in the comparison—only this time it was through her eyes alone and not through Ross's that she saw him.

The distant crying of the little boy floated down from an upstairs window as they walked out to the car. Zoë's heart clenched again as she pictured Ross leaning over the cot.

'You all right?' Clive was holding the car door open for her and saw the shadow of her feelings flicker across her face.

'Just a bit tired.' She managed to drum up a smile as she fastened her seatbelt. 'Ready to get away and work towards that holiday.' The words felt hollow but they pleased Clive.

He reached for her hand and squeezed it. 'That's my sensible girl. Damn them all, eh? We're going to head where the action is.'

Her hand felt totally unresponsive to his clasp. There

was no joy on Arran for her. She had no right to feel as she did about Ross and Jonathan. She had rejected this place and that man years ago. But what had she found to replace them? The world to which she was running away seemed an empty place. But 'sensible', Clive had said. And sensible she must be. Get on with her job. Have her holiday. Forget Ross and Arran.

'Wagons roll!' Clive said cheerfully, and started up the engine.

It was midnight when she had finished her packing. The phone, shrilling into the still night, startled her.

'I must see you again before you go,' Ross's voice said urgently.

'No, Ross,' she told him dully. 'Concentrate on your wife and child.' She wanted to hurt him because she was hurting. 'If you have anything else in mind, it's a game I don't play.' She put the phone down before he could answer, and he didn't call again.

CHAPTER FIVE

As LONG as they were caught up in the miles of driving and the buying fever Zoë found the time in France tolerable. While there were things to do, things that had to be kept at the forefront of her mind, pushing other thoughts into the shadows, she could function well, as she always did in her job.

The nights, though, were a different matter. It was then that she lay awake reviewing her life, going over the events of the day and seeing Clive as she never used to see him before her return to Arran.

Mid-week they called at a château where economic circumstances were forcing the gaunt, grey-faced owner to clear his cellars of supreme vintage wines laid down over the years before selling the château itself. Zoë was particularly moved by the experience, perhaps because she likened the French count and his castle to Ross Macallister and Innis Howe—and she knew only too well how unthinkable it had been for Ross to consider deserting his family's estate.

Clive shrugged carelessly when she voiced her feelings.

'If he hadn't gone bankrupt, we shouldn't have got the wine. It was probably meant for twenty-firsts and weddings and christenings for years to come—funerals too, and his looks not too far off. Ah, well, his loss is Elliot and Chalmers' gain. I can think of several of our plush clients who will lick their lips over that lot. So tough on Monsieur le Comte, but nice for them.'

Clive's blinkered attitude to the feelings and plight of anyone else seemed to hit Zoë at every turn now. He must have been always like this, she supposed, but she had accepted it uncritically in the cut-throat London business world where so many people had the same attitude. It was only now, after the clear light of Arran had fallen on Clive, that she was so aware of it.

One thing was beginning to emerge clearly from the events of the past two weeks. She was never going to feel any more for Clive than she did now. He could be fun, and he was quite good to work for, but on any more personal level he was not and never would be for her. Once this trip and the week in Cannes which she was committed to were over she would have to make that position clear to him. But tactfully if possible, because, whatever Ross had suggested, she had no real wish to change her job.

Ross. . . It was a mistake to have allowed him to slide into her thoughts again. That explosive revelation of her feelings when she found out he had a son—and found out how it affected her—still had the power to shake her. It was a bitter irony to find that what she had refused at the age of eighteen seemed to be what she most hopelessly longed for at twenty-four.

She must not think of Ross.

As they drove along the Croisette, the elegant sea-front road in Cannes, towards the high, dazzling white walls and twin domes of the Carlton where they were to spend the final week, Zoë acknowledged that this was going to be the most difficult, challenging time of the trip. And so it proved to be.

Three days which should have been perfect passed. The beach was only a step away across the Croisette. The view, from the crests of Estérel in the west of the bay to the emerald-green Isles de Lérins off the Pointe de la Croisette in the east, was wonderful. There were walks through the shady eucalyptus, pines and mimosas in the Bois de la Maure when the beach palled, wonderful meals in the seventh-floor gourmet restaurant at the Carlton, and everywhere the ever-changing, captivating scenario of fashionable holiday-makers to watch. Clive was at his most charming, attentive, affectionate, amusing. And yet. Zoë despised herself for it, but she couldn't stop herself from thinking constantly of a little northern island she had once hated and now seemed unable to forget.

Clive remarked on her preoccupation on the afternoon of the third day when they were sunbathing on the hotel's beach.

'The only thing that's wrong with this holiday, Zoë,' he said, looking lazily over her bronzed body and the kingfisher-blue bikini gracing it, 'is that while your body is undoubtedly here, as I'm not the only man to notice, your spirit certainly hasn't come along for the ride. What's wrong? When are you going to come clean about it? I've never known you moody like this.'

She rolled over and propped herself up on her elbows so that she could look across at him, realising guiltily that she had been lost in a brown study for ages and probably deaf to whatever he had been saying.

'What could possibly be wrong in a place like this?' she told him. 'I'm just getting dozy with all the sunshine. I need waking up a bit. Clive—what about going dancing tonight?'

He agreed with alacrity, asuring her that he would do anything that ensured her complete participation, and Zoë went back to the hotel, ostensibly to wash and pretty up her hair.

But once there she found herself dialling the number of Morag's shop, telling herself that she needed to check up on how things were going. What she really wanted to do, though, was to be in touch with Arran. There seemed to be a million invisible cords tugging her back to the island, no matter how hard she tried to ignore them.

Fiona's bright voice answered. 'Hello? Morag's store here.'

'Fiona—it's Zoë,' she said.

'Zoë! Where are you? You're surely not ringing from France?'

'Yes, from Cannes. I thought I'd better find out how things were going.' In her mind's eye Zoë could see the shore with its shining waters, feel the quietness so deep that you could hear a bee buzzing yards away.

'Much as ever. Nothing's going wrong with your arrangements, if that's what you're wondering. Donald's due in over the weekend for the shelving—and Catriona can't wait to be here. She's on the phone every day, as though she can't believe it. And guess who's in the shop right now? Ross! Perhaps he'd like a word too—oh!'

Zoë gave an involuntary gasp of protest, but over it she heard the sound of the shop bell backing Fiona's exclamation.

'Well—evidently the gentleman thinks not,' Fiona went on. 'His lordship's away without so much as a grunt in my direction. Zoë—the man's like a bear with a sore head these days. Heaven only knows what's got into him. He tore me off a strip yesterday when his wee pink paper hadn't turned up, as if I could help the boat not bringing it over.'

'I didn't want to speak to him, anyway,' Zoë was weak-kneed from knowing that Ross had been there in the shop, linked to her, whether he took it up or not, by Fiona's cheery but misguided offer of a word. She was now, no doubt, in his mind—though in no pleasant way after their last exchange on the phone—as he was in hers, whether she wanted him there or not.

'Just as well he didn't take me up on it, really. This

call must be costing a fortune without any extras. More fool me for suggesting one. I expect that's what Ross thought. So will I get off the line now?' Fiona chattered on.

Zoë pulled herself together. 'I'll call you when I'm back in London. And you have my number there, in any case, haven't you?'

'I have. Polly's missing you—though not enough to put her off her herring! Goodbye for now, Zoë, then.'

'*Au revoir*, Fiona.' Now why had she said that when she had no plan to see Fiona in the near future?

Zoë ached for Polly's silky, warm fur to stroke and find comfort in, but there was no likelihood of that particular hankering being satisfied. She reproached herself and got on with washing her hair; all the time, though, ghosts of Arran surrounded her until the effort she was determined to put into her appearance banished them.

She slipped on her white silk halter-neck dress and fastened the fine gold plaited belt. A slender gold chain and stud earrings comleted the look of understated elegance, but, when she turned, high on the back of her head there was an ornate gold-decorated Spanish comb studded with tiny brilliants anchoring her dark, silky hair before the gleaming length of it fell to the smooth brown skin of her back. It was the sort of eye-catching touch that Clive appreciated. She splashed herself liberally with the perfume he had given her at Christmas.

Surprisingly, the evening worked. Maybe it was because there was something in Zoë crying out for physical comfort. Whatever the reason, it was nice to have someone's arms round her, and she didn't draw away when Clive's face rested against hers as they danced. Nor did she object when he kissed her at the door of her room. It was a light, friendly kiss, and it had been a pleasant evening. She was pleased that she had actually enjoyed an hour or two of the holiday. That was progress.

It was this feeling of mild satisfaction that influenced her when Clive returned, minutes later, pushing a trolley with champagne on ice, a white cloth over his arm.

'Your nightcap, *mademoiselle*,' he said in an atrociously exaggerated accent, giving a flourish of the cloth. 'Such a happy night deserves a toast, *n'est-ce pas?*'

She hesitated, but it had been a good evening, and Clive looked so comically harmless. 'All right. Just a quick one,' she said, standing back.

As easily as that, mistakes were made. Zoë soon realised when they were out on her balcony that she had been a fool. Clive was pressed up against her on the chaise-longue, his intentions only too clearly moving on from the amusing stage. She made an excuse to get away from him and went to get a wrap from the bedroom, slipping into the bathroom which opened off her room to give herself time to work out a strategy which would get rid of Clive without leading to unpleasantness.

Clive was one jump ahead of her, though. When she unlocked the door he was standing in front of the dressing-table. He had taken off his white evening jacket, and he was unfastening his tie. He met her eyes in the tilted glass of the mirror and smiled like a cat knowing the saucer of cream was on its way.

'What are you doing, Clive?' Zoë asked, her pulse jumping with apprehension.

'Just getting rid of a few encumbrances.' He still didn't recognise what she was really feeling. He turned towards her and slid the angora jacket from her shoulders. 'Preparing, you might say, to celebrate the end of the ice age. Come on, sweetie. You're not going to need anything like this to keep you warm now, are you?'

She slipped away from him and went over to the door. 'You're assuming too much, Clive. I think you'd better go now.' Her hand was turning the knob, but he snatched it away.

'Oh—come on, Zoë. No going cold on me now. You asked me in, after all.'

She looked him straight in the eye. 'For a nightcap. Nothing more.'

There was dawning suspicion in his eyes that she just might be serious, but he had had plenty to drink, and he was not going to give in so easily, she recognised with a dreadful sinking feeling.

He tried to put an arm round her again. 'Come on. I've been patience itself this holiday, and you haven't been exactly shrinking away from me this evening. I know when a girl's enjoying being held.'

'Enjoying the dancing. I thought we both were.'

'Speak for yourself. Dancing's only an excuse. Everybody knows that. And you suggested it. You're a big girl now. You should know better than to spoil a pleasant evening.'

She held the door open. 'You're the one who's doing that. Please go now.'

She had once before seen him go white with rage during a disagreement with his partner. He reacted in exactly the same way now. There were no loud, vulgar outbursts from Clive when he was really aroused, but cold, concentrated venom, which was far, far worse.

He lowered his voice and proceeded to tell her in graphic detail exactly what he thought of her, using language that no one had ever spoken in Zoë's presence in a frighteningly controlled stream of scathing condemnation.

By the time he came to a pause, she was shaking with the sickening unpleasantness of it.

'And now perhaps you'll leave my room,' she managed to say.

'Perhaps I will,' he mocked savagely. 'But before I do, tell me how you're going to occupy yourself for the rest of the week while I seek more congenial company. Get yourself some bloody knitting? Because, believe me, I don't intend sitting on my backside with a maiden aunt for the next four days, of that you can be quite assured.'

She did then what it would have been far wiser to do the minute she realised that there was no future for her relationship with him.

'I'm not staying on here with you, Clive. And I'm not going to go on working for you. The impossibility of that is perfectly clear, I think. Please accept my notice. I shall fly home tomorrow and cut short the embarrassment for both of us.'

He walked over and snatched his jacket and tie off the bed. 'Do what you damned well like. Aim for the nearest nunnery. You should feel at home there. You haven't even got enough red blood in your veins to lose your temper, have you? What a po-faced little prude you are. This century wasn't made for such as you. I shall, of course, take care of the bill, for services rendered——' he looked her scathingly up and down '—strictly in the line of business.'

When he had gone, Zoë sat down on the bed, shaky and cold as reaction set in, her legs suddenly unreliable. She had written off the unproductive past, but what of the future? She had no job, no man, and her bridges were burned behind her. Where next? The future yawned ahead, bleak and empty.

Rock-bottom despair didn't hold her long. Soon she

realised that there was a glimmer of light in her mind, a light that had persistently flickered at intervals as she travelled through France. She thought about it, and the glimmer grew until Arran shone in her mind like a beacon. She needed time and space to think about her future. Arran would give her that. And she had responsibilities to see to—good reason for going back.

Yes. Morag had left her a storm, but she had also left her a haven. It was the haven that beckoned now, drawing her comfortingly towards it.

Three days later, after dealing with her affairs in London, Zoë drove up to Arran, this time taking her time and spending a night on the way.

When she turned into the farmyard at Innistulach, she found Fiona hanging out washing on the windy hillside. She came running down at once to greet Zoë.

'I had a kind of feeling you'd be back,' she told her. 'Don't ask me why. A sort of sixth sense, I suppose. You'll hardly recognise the shop. The shelves are in. Donald worked all weekend.'

'I'll look forward to seeing it tomorrow.' Zoë looked around, breathing in the clean air with its tang of the sea. 'Right now I'm ready to eat an ox. I missed out on lunch.'

'Seen your reception committee?' Fiona nodded towards Polly, waiting on the cottage doorstep. 'I think she knew you'd be coming too. She's kept hanging round the cottage apart from mealtimes, instead of moving in with us as she did before. I'll away and get bread and milk for you. Anything else?'

'If I get those, that'll be fine until morning,' Zoë said. 'There's enough tinned food to feed an army in there.'

She went round the cottage, eager to see and re-possess every room. What was it that Morag had said in

the words of the will? Something about hoping Zoë
would find happiness within its walls, and peace, and
tranquillity. She felt those qualities flowing gently into
her now. Perhaps it was only a welcome contrast to the
fast-moving days in France and the unpleasantness of
her break with Clive, but it felt like coming home, and
that was a feeling she hadn't experienced for years.

After they had eaten, Polly headed off up the hillside.
Zoë saw the golden eagles circling silently against the
rich blue of the sky. With an illogical desire to protect
the cat—who after all managed perfectly well on her
own, and was in any case probably far too heavy to be
snatched—Zoë ran after the bright marmalade fur.

'Hang on for an escort, Polly,' she said. 'I don't want
you being something's dinner.'

It was Polly who persisted in following the narrow
path up to the rocky seat in spite of all Zoë's attempts to
persuade her in another direction.

At least the place looked deserted. There was no one
sitting on the hollowed-out rock. Polly padded forward
and drew level with the stone, then sat on the heather,
tail tidily curled round, and suddenly a hand reached out
from the shelter of the rock to ruffle the bright fur. Zoë
froze.

'You again, wanderer,' a deep voice said softly. Ross's
voice. He must be sitting on the heather, using the rock
as a back rest.

Zoë stared as though hypnotised at his hand. She had
deliberately not thought about Ross, telling herself that
he was nothing to do with her, and had no part in her
decision to come back to Arran. But, as she watched the
movement of his long, sunburnt fingers over Polly's fur,
she knew that she had been deluding herself. Ross had
been as much the source of the force drawing her back
as Arran was. It was wrong that it should be so, but it

was true. And sooner or later she was going to have to come face to face with him without letting him know how she felt about him. So it might as well be now.

She stepped forward.

'Hello, Ross,' she said quietly.

His face changed from the affectionate look he had been directing towards Polly. His features were first wiped clean of any expression as he slowly got to his feet, then his mouth twisted ironically.

'You're the very last person I expected to see up here.'

'I decided to come back. There were things to be seen to. I felt as though I was ducking out of my responsibilities by not being here for the take-over at Morag's.'

'I'm impressed that you are taking your duties so seriously.'

'I intend to go on doing so,' she said with a touch of defiance, because he had spoken with something like sarcasm. She shrugged, 'So you'll have to get used to seeing me from time to time.'

'This isn't "from time to time", though, is it? It's only a matter of days since you were adamant you wouldn't be coming back.'

She tried to appear casual. 'Well. . .you know us women. I changed my mind.'

'Hm!' It was a brief sound but a sceptical one. She could feel him looking at her, trying to read her mind. 'How was the business trip?' Right to the point, like a lance through armour.

'Successful,' she said shortly.

'But brief.'

She felt like a butterfly on a pin. 'We did all we intended to do as far as business calls were concerned.'

'And yet you're back here so quickly. Do I take it that it was the week in Cannes that you cut short? Your "friend" seemed to set great store by it.'

She darted an angry glance at him, which was a mistake, because it let her see the conviction in his grey eyes that he knew exactly why she was back.

She aimed for the cool approach. 'Ferret away as much as you like, Ross. I fail to see why you should feel you have the right to grill me about the reason for my spending a little more time up here.'

'You're very fortunate that you have an employer understanding enough to grant you "a little more time" so hard on the heels of the days you took off for Morag's funeral.'

She succumbed, tight-lipped. 'If you must know, I now have no employer. And I can take as long as I like up here before finding myself another one.'

'I see.' She was expecting him to congratulate her on taking his advice, which she would deny emphatically. But he did no such thing. Instead he asked an unexpected question.

'And, having taken that step, how do you feel about it?'

'I feel all right. I shall feel better when I've got another job, though.'

'You could have sorted that out before handing in your notice.'

'But that's something you didn't advise me to do, isn't it?' She could have kicked herself for saying that. 'No— forget I said that. What you said had no bearing whatsoever on my decision.'

He ignored her words. 'A man like Clive, though, could have made life very unpleasant if he'd known you were looking elsewhere. What does he feel about your decision?'

'He has no choice but to accept it.'

'As your employer, yes. But as your "friend"?'

'Ross!' she said emphatically. 'Will you stop saying "friend" with that sneering question mark in your voice?'

'I'm more bemused than sneering. I never cease to marvel that someone of Clive's calibre, given the chance of a girl like you, doesn't grab her with both hands and stick a very identifiable label on her. However, there is a lot to be said for his not having done so.'

'You can drop all your snide remarks. Clive doesn't feature in my personal life either from now on. So his behaviour is irrelevant.'

'Thank the lord for that!' Ross said with feeling. 'I'm not going to pretend to be anything other than one hundred per cent delighted to hear it.'

'That doesn't surprise me. But let me say again, Ross—don't think you had anything to do with my decision. It was on the cards long before I met you again and had a surfeit of your opinions.'

'Whatever the reason, I'm whole-heartedly glad that you're not going to make the awful mistake I feared with your life,' he said. This time there was no sarcasm, no desire to score points, just quiet sincerity in his voice. Zoë looked at his strong, yet at this moment strangely tender face and felt an instant melting of the heart and a longing to take just one step closer to him and feel his arms hold her.

'You believe me?' he asked softly.

'I believe you.' Her voice shook. What was she doing—allowing herself to think thoughts like that about another woman's husband? If coming back to Arran was going to lead to weakness of that kind, then she was out of the frying-pan and into the fire. Was she the sort of fool who would never learn?

She took her one step—but backwards away from Ross.

The tenderness was wiped from his face instantly,

leaving him stern and cold. 'There's no need for that,' he said.

'I must go.' She avoided his eyes.

'Afraid again?'

'I don't know what you mean.'

'I think you do. But, if I have to remind you, you accused me of being a philanderer. You were wrong.'

'I would like to think I was—but you said things that no wife would enjoy hearing her husband say.' She looked at her watch and said pointedly, 'And right now your wife must be wondering where on earth you are.' She turned away and began to walk down the hill, knowing that there was danger here and she must get away from it.

'That presupposes that I still have a wife. . .' Ross said clearly and deliberately. The words were so unexpectedly startling that they stopped Zoë dead in her tracks. 'Yes—you heard correctly,' he went on. 'Don't run away again, Zoë. Come back here and listen, if you want an explanation of that. When you've had it, perhaps you'll stop seeing me as some kind of fool who can't survive a weekend of his wife's absence without developing a wandering eye. I should have told you all this before, I suppose, but I've got so used to shutting my mind to it. I know that I owe you an explanation, and I know equally that you owe me a hearing.'

There was a deadly seriousness about him that made it impossible to disobey. Zoë came slowly back.

'Sit down,' Ross said. He sat too, but not close to her, and Polly took advantage of the gap between them, turning round twice before curling herself into a neat cushion, nose to tail.

'I know you must have found me strangely uncommunicative about my marriage,' Ross began. 'All that interfering in your affairs. . .' he glanced down at her

'. . .and total silence on my own. Hardly fair, I can hear you thinking—with some justification.' He looked out over the Sound. 'If you have the patience to listen now, I want you to know exactly what kind of marriage I have. And for you to understand at all I must begin at the point where you left Arran five years ago. Bear with me if I seem to be going back further than necessary. It is all relevant.'

'You don't have to do this,' Zoë said quickly. 'I have no right to be curious about your life.' Mention of five years ago seemed dangerous, and she was suddenly afraid of what Ross was going to say.

He looked at her. 'I want to tell you,' he said simply. 'As long as you were going away and staying away, I didn't give a damn what you thought about me. What difference did it make? But if you're staying here a while, and maybe coming back often, then I'd rather not be misjudged.'

She made a little gesture of acquiescence. 'All right. Go ahead.'

'After you'd gone, and once you'd made your feelings quite clear by ignoring my letters, I put you out of my mind and threw myself into trying to drag the estate back from the edge of bankruptcy. The deeper I dug into the accounts, the greater the problems seemed to grow. It certainly focused the mind, but it was sad to feel that I might be going to lose Innis Howe despite all my resolution and efforts. Ironic, that would have been. And in fact it might well have come about if Alessandra's father hadn't stumbled across the estate on a working holiday he was taking.'

Alessandra. . . It was the first time Zoë had heard the name of Ross's wife. A soft, musical, beautiful name. A name to haunt a man.

'You know who Alessandra's father is?' Ross was asking.

Zoë shook her head. 'Morag only gave me the bare minimum of information in her letters.'

'He is Sergio Mellone, the film maker. American period films mainly. You may remember *In Faith They Sailed*, perhaps.'

'About the Pilgrim Fathers? Yes. I saw it,' Zoë said.

'Sergio was looking for locations, and when he saw Innis Howe he realised that it was just the kind of place he needed for his next film—not for any flattering reason. It was the right period and in the right state of dilapidation for his subject. The money he offered was staggering. It was enough to put an end to a great many of our problems. My parents moved over to a rented house on the mainland, and, in the light of what happened, never moved back. The film makers came. . .and with them came Alessandra.'

He paused, as though the musicality of the name recalled memories of their first meeting that were too demanding to hurry over.

'And you fell in love with her,' Zoë made herself prompt, trying to prove to herself that it didn't matter.

He nodded. 'She was—is—you'll understand the confusion of tense later—a beautiful girl. There was a freedom, a kind of tamed wildness about her that is difficult to describe. I was captivated by her—and I was not the only one.' Zoë felt blindly for Polly's warm fur. 'She had been a great wanderer—spent three years or so roaming around Europe and Asia—and she'd driven her family mad with worry in the process. Sergio was trying to involve her in the business and anchor her to that if not to one place. He was delighted when he saw the effect she had on me, and that Alessandra was equally attracted to me in return. I have never been able to understand how quickly it happened. It was like living in a constant high fever.' He looked down at Zoë as though trying to assess the effect of what he was saying. 'Do you find all this terribly boring?'

Painful, maybe, to hear how deeply he had felt for another woman so soon after her. Certainly the reverse of flattering. But boring—no. 'Not in the least. Go on,' she said quietly.

'I think that Sergio felt that marriage would solve all his problems with Aless—problems that I was far too blind to forecast for myself. From everyone's point of view there seemed every reason for an early marriage to be arranged. I was certainly as eager as anyone.' Again he looked at her. 'I'm trying to tell it exactly as it was— not make a Technicolor drama out of it.'

'Go on. . .' she said again.

'The wedding took place. The money from the filming along with Sergio's more than generous settlement on Aless allowed not only the renovation of Innis Howe, but also the establishing of the Trekking Centre and the holiday chalets. Life was full of change—and that suited Aless.' His expression changed, and Zoë could tell that the most difficult part of his story was coming up. 'But then fate stepped in. Aless discovered that she was pregnant. She raged against it. Children were a drag, a tie, an inhibiting factor in her book. She hated me, she hated the medical failure that had allowed her to become pregnant, and—what was worst of all—she hated the child she was carrying. At the same time there was something in her genes from the religion of her ancestors that prevented her taking drastic steps to change the situation. She just went on fighting a bloody war against it within the confines of her own body. I called in medical help, of course, but they achieved nothing to improve the misery of the physical progress of the

pregnancy nor to relieve Aless's tortured state of mind.
It was as though she was rejecting Jonathan before he
was born, and afterwards it grew worse. She sank into
the most deadly depression and would have nothing to
do with him. He was in the total care of nurses from the
outset.'

Zoë was appalled by the story. How deceptive appear-
ances could be. The shabby, older Innis Howe must
have seen infinitely more happiness than the apparently
bright and charming present house. Her heart ached for
Ross's child—and for Ross. She moved instinctively and
put out a hand to touch his.

'Oh, Ross. . .how absolutely awful it must have been
for all of you,' she said, her voice choked.

He didn't seem aware of her hand as he stared out
over the Sound, and, after a moment, she withdrew it.

'A pretty dark time,' he said. 'But the worst thing,
looking back, was that as the days went by and then the
weeks we almost accepted the situation as normal. Aless
improved, except where Jonathan and I were concerned.
She would go off riding and disappear for much of each
day. Jonathan stayed with his nurse. And I worked—
unremittingly. But of course it was all terribly wrong,
and it couldn't go on. Aless met up with a yachtsman—
an American who had put in to the island for a repair to
his boat. He was sailing wherever the fancy took him
round the world, and his stories must have fired her with
the first positive feelings she had had in ages. The old
wanderlust surfaced, and she told me that he needed a
crew member, and she had decided to go with him. She
couldn't face the future feeling as she did. She had to do
something to get her old zest for living back again.'

'You let her go with him?' Zoë said incredulously.
'And Jonathan only weeks old? Couldn't you have
stopped her?'

'I think I would have tried anything to get us back to
being a normal family again,' he said with feeling. 'But
as it happened I was not consulted until after the event,
in a manner of speaking. Aless told me of her decision in
a note, delivered to Innis Howe after the boat—*Trade
Winds*, it was called—had sailed.' His mouth twisted
with a mixture of anger and pain. 'Jonathan's name was
not so much as mentioned.'

Zoë was speechless. It was beyond her understanding.
The minor complications of her own life seemed nothing
in comparison with the chaos in Ross's.

'I just don't know what to say. . .' she said helplessly.

He turned blank grey eyes on her. 'That isn't the end
of the story. All that happened months ago. Several
weeks after Aless left, *Trade Winds* was found capsized
and badly damaged in the Pacific. There had been storms
of tremendous force. There was no trace of Aless, nor of
the man. Needless to say searches were carried out, and
not only by the authorities. We had men going over the
area for weeks, but they came up with nothing. Sergio
was distraught. It seemed a futile end to a life he had
hoped was set in happier lines at last.'

He fell silent, lost in his own dark thoughts, giving
Zoë time to realise that he had not said anything about
his own feelings. For herself, she had not known Aless
and had certainly not liked in the least what she had
heard about her, so she couldn't pretend to feelings of
overwhelming sadness. Ross, however, had loved Aless.
Deeply. He had left no doubt on that score. But could
he be—though not eager to admit it—relieved that his
awful marriage was over after the appalling way it had
deteriorated? Who could blame him? The idea grew in
her that it was so. It could only have been a relief, surely,
to be free of the tensions and horrors of what he had
gone through with Aless?

Suddenly the full implications of what Ross had told her made connections in Zoë's brain. Free! The word exploded in her like a bomb. Ross was not the married man she had thought him, then. Half ashamed of the paths her thoughts were following, she began to see glowing possibilities of second chances for herself. She had dazzling visions of fate having worked out her life for this moment when she could begin to make up to Ross for all he had suffered—and would not have suffered if she had not so misguidedly cut herself off from him. She felt that his silence was only preparation for the moment when he would turn to her with the old look in his eyes and say——

'Of course, for me it's not over. Far from it.' His voice brought her dreams crashing down. 'The Pacific is studded with islands. It's within the bounds of possibility that they were washed up on one our men didn't find. And people have been known to suffer injuries that affect memory.'

'Ross——' Again Zoë touched his hand. 'Is it wise to think on those lines?'

'That's the way the law thinks. As far as the legal position is concerned, Aless is missing and can't be presumed dead for seven years.'

Zoë's hopes of a magical happy ending faded. They had been foolish, selfish hopes in any case, at a time when her mind should have only thought of what Ross was feeling. Even so, if he had looked at her and asked her to wait until seven years had elapsed she would have gladly agreed. But he didn't ask her that. Instead he said, 'I hope you see now why I was so concerned that you should not find yourself in a marriage that brings such complications. I am probably over-sensitive on the subject—but with good cause.'

'I wish there was something I could say or do to help. . .' Zoë said unhappily.

He seemed to become fully aware of her at last, and gave her hand a pat such as would be given to a family pet. 'You have helped, in a way. Talking to you. . .telling you about it, has cleared my mind. I've been letting things ride for far too long. It's been easier in many ways with Aless gone—not having to live with that cloud of restless discontentment. . .not having to see how utterly uncaring about Jonathan she was. But to stop trying to do something about life is the coward's way out. I need to take action, as you did. I need a wife, and Jonathan needs a mother. Things can be worked out. Somtimes we are given a second chance. I shall reopen the search for Alessandra.'

Alessandra in full. That haunting name that seemed linked in his mind with the heady, wonderful days when he and his wife fell in love. His wife whom he still loved, as his last words had made painfully clear.

'I can't go on like this. . .' he said, and there was longing in his eyes.

It hurt to see love for Alessandra instead of the love for herself that she had deluded herself into hoping for. Zoë looked down at Polly, so that the sadness in her own eyes should be her secret, not Ross's embarrassment. Once again she had been a fool, and now she was suffering her punishment.

CHAPTER SIX

'I WISH I could say something to help.' Zoë looked up at
Ross when she was sure she was in control of herself. 'I
don't know how you have the heart to care a jot about
my affairs—or anyone else's. If there's anything I can do
to help. . . Oh! How futile that sounds in the light of all
you have to cope with. I mean it—but what can anyone
do?'

'I'm not looking for sympathy,' Ross said dismissively.
'My only purpose in telling you all this has been to clear
up any misunderstanding there may have been between
us.' He thawed a little. 'And you have already done quite
a lot by ensuring that I don't have to stand by and watch
you get yourself into a similar mess.'

No, not similar at all, Zoë thought. Different. Because
he was, in spite of everything, still in love with
Alessandra, and for her Clive might as well never have
existed. There was a world of difference between Ross's
feelings and her own.

'Nice to know I'm good for something,' she said, with
a half-hearted attempt at lightness.

He was in no mood to joke. 'I hope you realise,' he
said warningly, 'that I have told you all this in the
strictest confidence. People up here know the bare bones
of what's happened, but as you can imagine I'm not at
all eager to have them know the details of my domestic
situation. Helen comes from the mainland and spends
most of her time off over there, and my housekeeper
couldn't be more discreet. So there hasn't been much
chance for gossip.' He gave her a thoughtful, considering

look. 'So you see that I have trusted you with something very personal and close to me.'

Zoë's blue eyes blazed her reassurance. 'Don't worry. I shan't abuse your trust.'

'I'm sure you won't.' He ran a hand over Polly's fur, silent for a while. Then he asked, 'How long do you intend staying?'

'I really don't know. In fact—I don't know that I do want to go away at all. And that's a turn-up for the books, if ever there was one. I seem to have done a complete volte-face as far as Arran is concerned. It felt like coming home today. And Morag's cottage—well, it *fits* me, if you know what I mean. And so far I've no reason to leave.'

'What about little things like earning a living?'

'You told me I was privileged, didn't you? I suppose I am. If I wanted to live on my resources for a bit I could certainly do that.'

'What about the boredom factor? Your life has been fairly dynamic these last few years.'

Zoë shrugged. 'You can lose the taste for that. And in any case there's plenty I can do here. The reorganisation of the shop for one thing. I've got several ideas to talk over with Catriona when she moves in.'

'A sophisticated restructuring of Morag's, city-style?'

They laughed. 'Not quite that,' Zoë said.

Ross stretched. 'Well, as a matter of fact I would rather like it if you stayed on. A friendly ear would be a great help from time to time. Mixing socially is rather a problem for a man in my position. There's no point in anyone getting the idea that I'm available—but I don't want the distasteful task of explaining just how unavailable I am—and for how long. It would be nice to have someone around who knew the score.'

'I suppose that's why you come up here so much,' Zoë said.

'I have a long-standing attachment to this place, as you know. And it's an escape from four walls. I don't do much entertaining at Innis Howe for reasons you now know.'

'You entertained us.'

'That was entertaining with a purpose.'

Polly stirred, and Zoë picked her up. 'I suppose I'd better get this one back indoors. I was afraid of the eagles.'

'They wouldn't get her. Not with a corporation like that.' He poked Polly in the tummy, and his eyes met Zoë's. 'Will you come and talk to me again? I would enjoy that. . .and I could let you know how the search is going.'

She contemplated the exquisite pain of being informed of every stage of his search for Alessandra and his feelings about it.

'If you like. . .' she said.

He picked up the doubt in her voice. 'You needn't be afraid of my stepping out of line in any way. I know you suspected me of that. I'm far too aware of all the possibilities to give way to any such idea. I know that if Aless is alive, and came back with a change of heart about Jonathan but the same feelings for Innis Howe and therefore for me, the way I behave could weigh either for me or against me in a custody battle. God forbid that the latter should happen. So you can be sure that I shan't embarrass you.'

'I'm not exactly Victorian!' Zoë protested.

'There's nothing Victorian about having principles.'

'That's an opinion you definitely don't share with Clive.' She pulled a face at the memory of the tirade she would rather like to forget.

'I wouldn't brood over any thoughts of Clive,' Ross said.

'Don't worry. I shan't,' she told him confidently.

But there was plenty to brood about in bed that night— none of it concerning Clive.

It was some kind of consolation to feel that Ross cared enough about her to be glad of her company, as well as wanting her life to work out more satisfactorily than his own had done. And he had more or less asked for her help. That made her want to give him as much support as possible.

Could she bear to do that, though, feeling as she did about him? And knowing how he felt about Alessandra in spite of everything?

'Could I, Polly?' she asked the cat, who had taken advantage of her preoccupation to curl up on the duvet at her feet for the night. 'It wouldn't be easy. . .'

But it would at least be worthwhile. More so than any alternative offering itself at the moment. The London rat race and the plastic people flashed distastefully into her mind. Here there were real people, with real needs. It might do her a power of good to forget what she wanted for herself, and concentrate on making life better for someone else. Looked at one way, she had, through her own immature selfishness all those years ago, opened a way into Ross's life for a sea of troubles. Her conscience wouldn't let her forget that, even if she went miles away, so she might just as well stick around and do what little she could to help the situation.

Zoë was not a fool. She knew that if she were not to develop too close and dangerous a relationship with Ross she had to fill her life with plenty of other interests, and this she at once set about doing.

Once Catriona arrived, plans for the shop began to take shape. Quite a bit of time was devoted into transforming the terrace in front of the shop entrance into a garden table area for self-service refreshments. A more reliable van was tracked down and bought so that a delivery service could be started—something that Zoë herself would be involved in as a way of getting to know people. One way and another, every day was filled with activity.

It was usually in the evenings that she saw Ross. He would now and again knock on the cottage door when he was going over to the seat, and ask if she was coming too. Zoë was careful to find the occasional diplomatic reason for not going, both to test herself and to keep the temperature between them on a moderate level. Secretly, though, she treasured the time they spent talking up there. It was like the old days. Like, and yet poignantly different.

Ross told her that he had sent men to search again in the area of the Pacific where it was feasible that Alessandra could be. When she heard the number of islands to be covered, Zoë said, 'It must be costing you a fortune!'

'It's worth every penny,' he said simply. 'I couldn't go on like this now. We've got to know *something*, one way or the other.'

In the same sentence he had both brought her close and distanced her. '*We've* got to know something,' he had said, as though she were as involved in the desire to find Alessandra as he was. But his determination to spare no expense, to go to any lengths in the search for his wife, left Zoë where she really was—the outsider, the stop-gap friend whose function would no longer exist once he had found Aless again.

There were happy times, though, when she managed almost to forget the hopelessness of her feelings for Ross.

Invitations started to trickle in from all over the island. Ross would check that she was included, and accept for himself where once he would have refused. And always he would gravitate towards the safety of her side. People seemed to accept them as friends, almost as a couple. Only, of course, Zoë and Ross knew that this was something they were not. There might be times of pleasure, but Zoë was always brought back to reality.

Things were not always easy. She had known it would be like that. One particular evening at a dance over in Brodick was dodgy from the start, and finished positively explosively.

Ross called to pick her up, and when Zoë ran downstairs in her silver-grey dress with its feminine neckline and big sleeves he complimented her on her appearance.

'You look lovely, Zoë. . .' He was not given to personal remarks of that kind, and he added, 'But I'm sure your mirror has told you that already,' as though wanting to generalise the opinion.

'You look rather good yourself!' she said. He was wearing his dress tartan, flattering to any man but on a good-looking specimen of Ross's build devastatingly dashing. 'Mrs Lewis will think she has made a fine pair of us.'

Ross looked at her. 'What do you know of what Mrs Lewis thinks?'

Zoë told him light-heartedly, ignoring the warning lights. Mrs Lewis was the lady who was organising the ball, and in whose house it was held. She was a sweet old matchmaker, but perfectly harmless.

'Oh—she said it would be a great kindness if I would look after you, then she wouldn't have to worry about you.'

Ross's face darkened. 'Pretty much what she said to me. Why doesn't the patronising woman mind her own

business? I am perfectly capable of organising things for
my own convenience.'

'I thought that was exactly what you had done.' Zoë
was rather piqued to be put in the convenience category.
'Am I not supposed to be the buffer between you and all
these panting women?'

'Interfering old Lewis doesn't know that, does she?'

Zoë picked up her bag. 'She doesn't mean any harm,
Ross. Don't be unreasonable.'

'The amount of harm done by people who mean none
is quite staggering,' Ross said grimly. 'However, I'm
sure we shall find a way to show our friend a thing or
two tonight.'

Zoë wasn't sure what he meant by that and preferred
not to enquire. With a bit of luck Ross's annoyance
would have evaporated by the time they got to the Dial
House.

Just before they reached the Lewis's house, Ross asked
how things were going with her business venture.

'Very well. Apart from my doing the late afternoon
deliveries which Catriona can't get involved in, the place
is ticking over nicely now.'

'If you're looking for something else to do, I might
have an offer to make,' he said.

'What kind of offer?'

'I've been thinking for some months that we could
feature riding for the disabled holidays. But I haven't
had time to do all the research necessary. If you were
interested in looking into it for me, I could find office
space for you at the Trekking Centre.'

Zoë didn't answer at once. It would mean seeing more
of Ross. Could she cope with that? 'You've rather taken
me by surprise,' she said eventually, hedging.

'It isn't the sort of extra I could ask one of our girls to
do. It needs someone used to making contacts and

following up leads. I'd appeciate your help. Think about it, will you?'

'All right. . .' she said slowly. 'I will.'

Zoë had a couple of dances with Ross, then, rather to her surprise, he excused himself, saying something about one or two duty dances.

'You'll be all right?' he asked, though clearly expecting an affirmative answer.

'Oh—perfectly!' She waved to someone she knew, and didn't watch as he walked away.

She did watch surreptitiously, however, and with the most humiliating worm of jealousy gnawing away inside her, when she saw Ross walk out on to the floor with a far too attractive blonde, who looked anything but a duty partner from the way she draped herself around him.

Zoë's reaction to this was to step up her own response to the man she was dancing with, who must have wondered what strange power he had suddenly developed to have this beautiful young girl hanging on his every word, looking up at him with blue eyes he could easily have drowned in.

Her animation brought partners buzzing round, and it was not until the supper dance that Ross managed to claim her again.

'My dance, I think,' he said curtly, whipping her away from John Blakely, who had a bit of a reputation and with his wife away in hospital was on the loose.

Ross didn't speak for a while, and neither did Zoë. Then he said shortly, 'You know Blakely is married?'

'I do,' Zoë said lightly. 'So does everyone else here, I imagine.'

'I'd advise you to watch your step with him.'

'Oh—I shall. But I find him quite refreshing to be

with. He's not afraid to enjoy himself—and he doesn't give a fig for what the world thinks.'

'What exactly do you mean by that?' He was sweeping her round the floor at such a pace that she could hardly match her steps to the length of his.

'Just what I say. He's uncomplicated. You know exactly what he's up to—and that in a way makes him harmless. I'm sure his wife understands him perfectly!'

'A pity I dragged you away from such fascinating company,' he said icily.

'You can always take your blonde friend in to supper if you prefer.' She gave him a carefree, dazzling smile that was totally false.

'Don't be ridiculous. I brought you to the dance. I wouldn't dream of taking anyone else in to supper.'

'How very correct!' She sailed ahead of him into the supper-room as the music stopped, and filled her plate with food that she had no idea how she would manage to eat, and Ross followed along the buffet table behind her, looking as though he would rather have a good fight with someone than sit down for a civilised meal.

Fortunately other people joined them at the table and they sat in a jolly group to eat. Zoë felt as jolly as a funeral guest but hid her feelings under continuing effervescence. She knew she was being silly, but she was so angry with herself for feeling jealous about Ross and the blonde that she would have gone to any lengths to prove to him what a good time she was having. The sane, rational part of her knew that she hadn't the least right in the world to be in such a mood. Ross had been absolutely straightforward with her. She was going to regret this later. But she couldn't stop herself.

She talked brightly to the man next to her, and took a certain satisfaction in going off to dance with him when the music started up again. She avoided Ross until the very end of the evening when he caught up with her for the last dance.

'I didn't expect such childish behaviour from you,' he said grimly, his voice at odds with the slow, sentimental music.

'I don't know why you should consider it childish for me to fit in with your desire to show Mrs Lewis that there's no romance for her to foster. She should have no illusions left by now,' Zoë said.

'Don't be so ridiculous. All that was necessary was for us to have the occasional dance with someone else. You didn't have to go off in a strop for the whole evening.'

'I didn't. I was thoroughly enjoying myself.'

'Liar! You were spitting venom every time we met. That sickly smile didn't fool me for an instant.'

'Oh—shut up!' Zoë said ungraciously, and they finished the dance in stony silence.

Mrs Lewis must have seen that there was no danger of ruining a cosy drive home for two by inflicting a passenger upon them, because she stopped them as they left the floor to ask if they would be so kind as to take a fellow guest home.

'It's young Martin McGregor, and he's on your route,' she said apologetically, lowering her voice to add, 'He's indulged rather more than is wise, and I think his car will be safer here until tomorrow.'

'It'll be a pleasure,' Zoë said before Ross had the chance to answer.

'Of course. No trouble at all,' Ross said with cold courtesy.

From the set of Ross's jaw on the drive home Zoë knew that she didn't want to be left alone with him, so she made sure that he drove her up to Innistulach before dropping off the garrulous young McGregor, whose cheerful chattering had covered up the ominous silence between herself and Ross.

Ross, however, wasn't going to let her get away so easily. He strode after her through the cottage gate on the pretext of seeing her in safely.

'I haven't cared for your mood tonight,' he said at the door.

'Haven't you?' She affected surprise. 'Nobody else has complained.'

'To hell with your other partners. I'm talking about your objectionable attitude towards me.' The fact that he was talking in undertones to avoid McGregor's over-hearing didn't detract in the least from the force of his annoyance. Zoë felt a vicious sense of triumph.

'Gosh! I'm so tired!' She yawned exaggeratedly. 'Can we leave all this, Ross? I'm too bushed tonight to know what you're on about, in any case.'

'You mean you're too pig-headed to admit to what you've been up to. Very well. Perhaps you'll have come to your senses when I see you tomorrow.'

'Oh—not tomorrow,' she said sweetly. 'I've been asked to go out for an evening sail. Sorry.'

'If it's John Blakely, you're a fool!'

'No. It's not John Blakely,' she said. But she didn't tell him who it was.

'I hope it keeps bloody well fine for you,' he flung at her, and turned on his heel to give Martin McGregor— if he had been sober—the most hair-raising hurtle down the track.

Elation at having really got under his skin wafted Zoë into the cottage and up to her room before depositing her with a thump on the ground again.

What on earth was she playing at? She had absolutely no justification for her behaviour, which stemmed from the fact that the first two dances with Ross had been so

lovely that she would have asked for nothing more
delightful than to spend the rest of the evening dancing
with him. She knew perfectly well that that way danger
lay. Ross—ever sensible—had been prepared to have
the odd dance with someone else but spend the bulk of
the evening with her. She had cut off her own nose to
spite her own silly face.

She sat on the edge of the bed and snivelled a bit
about it, but it was too damned silly to get in too much
of a state about. An evening to write off in the name of
experience.

If it had proved anything, though, it was that if she
was capable of letting her feelings for Ross surface in
this humiliating way then she certainly couldn't cope
with working for him and the increased contact that
would mean. She must tell him so—and find some
credible excuse for her behaviour tonight. And she'd
make a peace-offering of some kind. She would get him
information about riding for the disabled in her spare
time, maybe. There was someone she had been at college
with whose aunt had run a stable operating the scheme.
She would be a good starting point.

Zoë finally went to bed, very sober, very penitent, and
very full of good intentions.

Fiona, who was now doing her summer replacement job
at the Bell Rock, came over on her way home from work
the following afternoon.

'Got a minute to spare?' she asked Zoë.

'As many as you want until six-thirty. Have a cup of
tea?'

'Love one.' Fiona followed her into the kitchen. 'You
seem to be staying on.'

'I do, don't I?'

'What happened to the classy job at the wine merchant's?'

'I scrapped it.'

'And the wine merchant himself, too?'

'Spot-on.'

Fiona grinned. 'Well—you don't seem exactly heart-broken, so I won't sympathise. And I'm not just being nosy. I'm really sounding you out before putting an offer to you. Alec asked me to see you on the quiet. If you really are staying, and if you need a term's work—only part time—there's some secretarial work going at a school in the south of the island. Is that an insult?'

'Of course not. Tell me more.'

The full-time secretary has a slight heart condition, and her doctor wants her to cut down temporarily. She'd like to keep three days and farm out two. The head's a very decent sort. But they'd want to be sure of your staying for the full term until Christmas. Would you be interested?'

'I think I would. . .' Zoë said thoughtfully. It would give her a valid excuse for not taking up Ross's offer, for one thing. Someone's health was at stake, and that had to count for her, surely? 'Yes. I definitely would,' she amended.

'Good. Then phone this number tonight, will you?' Fiona handed over a scrap of paper. 'It's the head's home, and if he hears from you he won't advertise. And now let's have that tea!'

It was a couple of days before Zoë saw Ross again, by which time the part-time job at the school was fixed. He seemed quite unoffended, almost pleased about it. Maybe he too had had second thoughts about the wisdom of his suggestion that she should work for him. Neither of them mentioned the evening of the dance, so second and wiser thoughts prevailed in that area too.

'But I'm trying to get you some information about your riding for the disabled scheme,' she added, telling him about her college friend.

'That sounds like a bargain for me. I was intending paying you for doing it,' he protested mildly. 'Tell you what—at least let me give you lunch at Innis Howe when you hear from your friend. Jean will enjoy cooking for someone else for a change, and Helen will like a bit of young female company.'

He was telling her that there would be plenty of people around as well as Jonathan, but she didn't mind about that. She was just glad that the unpleasantness of the Lewis's dance had blown over. She would have to be very careful that it didn't happen again.

After that initial visit, Saturday lunch at Innis Howe became quite a regular affair. Zoë got on well with Helen. Sometimes she would spend part of the afternoon alone with her and Jonathan, if Ross had pressing matters to see to.

The summer weeks were turning out not to be as hard as Zoë had feared. She was finding that life could have a richness of texture without the excitement of London's theatre and night life. Arran had its own highlights. There were concerts in Brodick Castle, the Highland Games, sheepdog trials, and an infinity of private social occasions. There was, too, the constant discovery of the richness and fascination of the flora and fauna of the island against the changing physical beauty of the place under all kinds of skies and in all kinds of weather.

There were, of course, times when Zoë felt that she was paying a high price for staying on. Twice she was at Innis Howe when Ross took phone calls from the people carrying out the systematic search for news of Aless. It was painful to see the spark of hope that flared in him as they first spoke fade away to resigned depression or frustrated anger as there continued to be no results. Zoë's own reaction was directly opposed to his—dread at the prospect of Aless being found, relief when there was no news. She was highly self-critical about her feelings, but that was how things stayed.

Jonathan quickly charmed his way into her heart. He knew her now, and stretched out his arms to her when he saw her. There was even the first mini-tantrum she had seen him have one Saturday, when he didn't want her to go.

The next week Helen and Jonathan were missing.

'Where are they?' Zoë asked, looking round eagerly.

Ross avoided her eyes. 'Gone to the beach.'

'Oh!' Disappointment was in her voice. 'Couldn't they have gone some other day? I look forward to seeing Jonathan. And he likes seeing me.'

'I know he does.' There was something in his voice that made her look at him suspiciously.

'I believe you deliberately sent them away today, didn't you?'

'I'm afraid I did.' He came over to her, his grey eyes worried. 'Please don't be hurt, Zoë. It's just that after Jonathan made such a fuss when you were leaving last time I got cold feet and wondered what I was doing with his affections. He's really been mucked around enough. Is it fair to let him get fond of you when we don't know. . .?' His voice tailed away. 'I'm sorry,' he added after a moment.

The joy seeped out of Zoë's day. He was right, of course. They didn't know how long she would be around. She was not a permanent fixture at Innis Howe.

'Is that how it's going to be from now on, then?' she asked, her voice subdued.

'I think it would be wiser.'

'Would you rather I didn't come to the house?'

'No. I value your company.' He spoke with some urgency. 'Next week Jonathan will be away, without any scheming on my part, I promise. Helen's taking a week's holiday and my parents are having their grandson on the mainland. I'll be going across to deliver him, but the following Saturday he won't be brought back until evening. I wondered if you'd like to have a ride up the Glen with me and take a picnic. I need to check on the water level in the high loch up there. It would be something different. Jean is away that weekend, too,' he added casually.

And of course he wouldn't ask her to the house with no one else there. Oh, wise, rock-solid Ross. How the more reprehensible side of her longed for him to forget himself and behave like a weaker, lesser man. And how good a thing for both of them it was that he was so strong. Zoë accepted his invitation without too much enthusiasm, then fortunately Jean announced lunch at that point, and saved the atmosphere from sinking any lower.

The day of the planned ride was gloriously hot. Wondering if they would swim in the loch, Zoë put a white bikini on under her checked cotton shirt and thin trousers. Ross was wearing a sleeveless dark blue vest with his jeans, and as she followed him along the single track Zoë thought guiltily that being on the back of a horse seemed to stir up similar thoughts to being in the back of a car. She kept looking at Ross's broad, sun-tanned shoulders, consumed by the most maddening desire to touch them.

Oh—snap out of it! she told herself, and made a determined effort to take an interest in their surroundings.

'A penny for them?' Ross called over his shoulder, aware of her quietness.

'They're worth a good deal more than that,' she said, 'but I'm not going to share them with you.'

The picnic was only a moderate success. The cold chicken and salads with crusty bread Ross had brought for them both were delicious, and they had a sparkling white wine cooled in the stream that ran into the loch. But they were a little uneasy with each other all the time. Ross was probably regretting having brought her up here with no one else for miles around, Zoë thought. And she seemed incapable of snapping out of her illicit subconscious. A swim might have been a good idea, but the combination of sun and wine was in any case stupefying, and Zoë couldn't be bothered to suggest it.

Ross seemed to have fallen asleep, she realised after a pause in the not-very-spirited conversation about an insignificant little plant growing in the roots of the grass and heather. It was called bedstraw, and Zoë felt that she now knew more than she ever wanted to know about it. She opened her eyes and saw that Ross was breathing slowly and regularly.

She propped herself up on her elbow and allowed herself a rare, undisturbed look at him. His head was pillowed on his upflung arm, his lashes thick on his cheek, and his mouth relaxed and tempting in sleep. She hardly ever saw him when he wasn't utterly controlled, or keyed up against some task or issue, and now he had an almost vulnerable look that made her want to lean closer and closer to him.

But she mustn't. Why do I have to love you? she asked herself silently.

At that moment he awoke and looked straight into her eyes. Not just into her eyes, though, but, it seemed, into her mind and her heart. For a second they stared at each other, while all the suonds of the hillside seemed to fade away into a spellbinding silence.

Then Ross groaned and reached out for her, pulling her roughly towards him so that both of them fell back against the heather. It was transformed instantly into a soft, scented bed, full of heady allure, full of danger.

With feverish abandon they rolled to and fro on the purple bell flowers, Ross's weight now crushing Zoë beneath him, now pulling her on top of him in a frenzy of kissing and caressing until they were both flushed and panting as Ross halted to look down into her glowing face.

She saw the fire in his eyes die as she looked at him, and he scrambled to his feet and stood with his back towards her, fighting for control.

'I had no right to do that,' he said, his voice tight with strain. 'I've been feeling like an animal all day—knowing I was up here alone with you. Now I've behaved like one, and I had no right. . .no right at all to subject you to all that.' He turned round and looked at her again. 'I'm doing my damnedest to find Aless and end this hellish situation. I pride myself on my self-control, but I couldn't have given a worse demonstration of lack of it. What can I say? If it makes you any more inclined to forgive me, I think I had been dreaming. Even my damned subconscious works against me, curse it.'

Zoë was sitting up straightening her clothes, trying to come to terms with the knowledge that she had only been the echo of a dream of Aless, when for one miraculous moment she had deluded herself that Ross felt more than friendship for her.

'No great harm done,' she said, her tone as matter-of-fact as she could make it. 'I've had far worse experiences. Let's forget it, shall we?'

'As easily as that?' He looked as though he loathed himself and her for what had happened. Was the thought of having kissed and held her really so repugnant to him?

'Well, what else do you suggest? A wake, because you acted like a normal man instead of like a bronze god for once?' she said, anger growing inside her.

'Is that what you think of me?'

'Oh, you, you, you! Forget yourself for once, Ross.' She got up with determination. 'Let's do something and take our minds off that appalling fall from grace. Have a swim. Why not?'

'I have no desire for a swim,' he said stuffily, turning to look out over the loch.

Something in Zoë snapped. She came up behind him at speed.

'Well, you bloody well need one!' she shouted, pushing hard with both hands in the small of his back, and the craggy sides of the Glen threw back an echo over the splash as Ross hit the water of the loch. 'Need one. . .need one. . .need one. . .'

She felt a brief flood of satisfaction, then, when he did not immediately surface, triumph gave way to panic. From where she was, the sun was so bright and dazzling on the pool that she couldn't see anything in its depths, and Ross had told her how deep some of these high lochs were. Visions of hidden rocks and of Ross's head crashing on them horrified her. She crouched on the edge, straining to see, calling his name as the ripples washed ever more slowly outwards from the point where he had hit the water.

Suddenly, he broke the surface near her, and a hand

reached up to catch the arm she was leaning on and bring her toppling head first into the water with him.

'Two can play that game,' he said viciously, pushing her under again when she came up, gasping and spluttering, and fighting back her long dark hair.

She surfaced again. 'Pig!' she hurled at him, sending a shower of water into his mocking face.

'Pig yourself!' he retorted, doing likewise.

Zoë dived and swam away underwater. Ross followed, an infinitely more powerful swimmer than she was, and as they swam a miracle happened. The tension that had been between them melted away in childish horseplay that set the peaks ringing with echoes of their laughter.

Before long Ross hoisted himself out on to the slab of rock at the end of the loch and began to strip off his jeans and trainers.

'Better get yours off too and let them start drying. Since we appear to be swimming, we may as well do it properly. Rex and Taffy aren't going to appreciate wet backsides once we get going again,' he called to Zoë.

She joined him and spread out her own cotton trousers beside his on the rock that was burning hot to her bare feet.

They dived in again, and this time, unencumbered by footwear and clinging fabric other than the briefest of garments, they were able to revel in the velvety softness of the water. Deep down it was icy cold still, but the surface water where the sun's rays had penetrated was glorious. Eventually they floated side by side with eyes closed against the dazzling light and really talked, instead of the pathetic 'making conversation' that had gone on before.

I shall remember this time always, Zoë thought as they rode back down the Glen. Whatever happens, good or bad, this hour will be like a jewel in my memory. The loch and the heather, and the blue, blue sky. . .and the brief time when Ross and I actually had fun together and forgot the rest of the world.

Helen was collecting Jonathan from his grandparents' house and returning on the six o'clock ferry, so Zoë was going straight back to the cottage once they had returned the horses.

Ross came into the stall where she was unsaddling and rubbing down Taffy. There was no one else around. The trekking parties were still out.

'Thank you, Zoë,' he said simply. 'Thank you for turning a bad time into an unforgettable one.'

She smiled up at him, relieved that they were once again on safe ground. 'You make me sound a right little miracle-worker!'

'Some day, I hope, you'll get your reward.' He looked as though he really meant that.

'I hope so,' she told him. But it wouldn't be the reward she wanted. As so often happened these days, the day turned to ashes.

Late that night, unable to sleep, Zoë was trying to read in bed when the phone rang, far too late for a normal call.

She could tell at once from Ross's voice that something was badly wrong.

'Zoë—can I ask you to come over to Innis Howe? As quickly as you can?'

CHAPTER SEVEN

'WHAT'S wrong?' Zoë asked, already sitting on the edge of the bed.

'It's Helen. She's ill—very. And I'm stuck here on my own. I've got to get her to hospital. Appendix, I suspect, but I'm no expert. She didn't manage to say too much before she passed out. Quite frankly, I daren't hang on for an ambulance. It looks as though every second might count. But I can't leave Jonathan alone, and it wouldn't help to take him with us the way things are. You were the first person I thought of calling.'

'I'll be over right away,' Zoë said, on her feet and reaching for clothes with her free hand already.

'Thanks, Zoë. Be careful, but be quick. I'll be ready for off the minute you get here.'

Zoë whipped off her nightdress and pulled on trousers and a shirt, then, snatching her keys out of her handbag, she ran downstairs and out of the cottage, staying neither to put off lights nor close the door behind her. She drove as quickly as she could down the track and along the silent dark coast road, then up the ghostly Glen to Innis Howe.

Ross was carrying out a moaning Helen to place her gently on a makeshift bed he had arranged in the back of the Range Rover. The back seat which he had taken out was flung on the drive, and in its place were a mattress and duvet. The girl looked ghastly in the light of Zoë's headlamps. Her forehead was running with sweat and her complexion livid. Zoë saw that it was useless to try to speak to her. It was patently obvious that she was barely conscious and way beyond anything like good wishes.

'Ring the hospital, will you?' Ross said hurriedly as he climbed into the driving seat. 'Tell them we're on our way—they may have to get in touch with a surgeon. And say it's abdominal pain, fever, vomiting. I'll ring you as soon as I can.'

The Range Rover roared into life, but he moved off carefully down the drive. Zoë thought of the half-hour or more journey ahead of him, and hoped nothing awful would happen on the way. Helen had looked so very ill. She dragged the car seat over to the side of the drive, out of the way for when Ross returned, and then went in quickly to look up the hospital's number.

The duty officer who answered sounded professionally calm and reassuring. 'I'll start the wheels turning here. Someone will ring you as soon as there's something to report. Don't worry. We specialise in emergencies—and it certainly helps to know one is coming and what kind it's likely to be.'

The phone call made, Zoë turned to her next priority—to see that Jonathan was all right. There was no sound from upstairs, so presumably he had slept through the drama. She realised that though she had been here often she had no idea which was his room, and went quietly upstairs to investigate.

The first open door she encountered was obviously Ross's room. Clothes of his were lying around.

The next room to his had a closed door. She opened it cautiously but the light from the corridor showed that it was a spare bedroom. Two more unoccupied bedrooms followed, and a bathroom, then another room with an open door. Helen's room, immaculately tidy apart from the disturbed bed, the dress the girl had obviously intended wearing tomorrow lying over a chair with clean

underwear neatly folded. Zoë swallowed, hoping desperately that the suddenly pathetic clothes would be worn
again, and that whatever it was that was making their
owner so ill, so suddenly, could be dealt with. The bed
would have to be made and probably changed since there
was a smell of sickness in the air. But she would see to
that later.

Beyond Helen's room, at the back of the house, was
Jonathan's nursery. A lamp in the form of a cottage with
soft light glowing in its windows was burning, and by its
faint illumination Zoë could see that the little boy was
sound asleep, lying on his stomach, surrounded by a
tangle of bedclothes and soft toys.

Carefully she covered him, thinking how beautiful the
sleeping child looked, and feeling as she did each time
she saw him what an outrage it was that his mother
should have been so completely indifferent to him.

She stayed there in the dim light for a moment,
looking at the room now that her eyes were adjusting.
This was Ross's work, obviously, since no one else had
cared enough to create a happy atmosphere for the child.
There was a mobile of fluffy sheep over the cot, and she
could make out others with birds and fishes and charac-
ters from 'Winnie-the-Pooh' in different parts of the
room. A frieze of teddy-bears marched at child height
round the walls, and child-sized furniture in bright
colours was waiting for Jonathan to be big enough to use
it. Shelves with shadowy shapes of soft toys on them
filled one wall, and there was already quite a row of
books on which the light from the landing fell. Zoë
pictured Ross buying them alone, anxious to make up to
his son for the deprivation that was no fault of his,
moving years ahead with Peter Rabbit and Pooh and
Piglet, Raymond Briggs' Snowman, Rupert Bear—a
well-thumbed copy this, and perhaps dating from Ross's
own childhood.

Quietly she tiptoed out of the room and closed the door. It was a bitter-sweet place.

Back in Helen's bedroom, the bedclothes, damp from the raging fever she had been in, were soon changed for fresh sheets from a linen-room on the opposite side of the corridor. Zoë opened the window to air the room before taking the dirty linen down to leave in the laundry beyond the kitchen.

She felt wide awake and restless, unable to settle down until Ross called. She made coffee and filled a flask for him, then found cold chicken in the fridge and cut sandwiches. He would probably feel like something to eat when he got back, if all had gone well.

In the sitting-room she tried to read without much success, and resorted to prowling round the ground floor of the house, absorbing Ross's territory as she could never satisfactorily do when he was there. At last the phone shrilled, and she hurled herself at it.

'Are you all right?' Ross asked.

'Fine. Jonathan's sleeping like an angel. How are things with you?'

'Nothing definite to report yet. They're operating right now. Seems that it is Helen's appendix, though they won't know the extent of the trouble until they get her opened up. Their delicate phrase, by the way, not mine.'

'Poor Helen,' Zoë said with feeling. 'And poor you. I guess it was a relief to hand over the responsibility to someone else. How was the journey?'

'Not one I'm anxious to repeat. I don't think Helen was aware of much, but she was moaning most of the time. I just kept going as carefully as I could, hoping to hell that I was doing the right thing.'

'Which you obviously were. If they're operating right away it must be urgent. Will you be staying there?'

'Yes, until I know what's happened. Is that all right by you?'

'Perfectly. Don't worry about Jonathan.'

His voice softened with a warmth that went to the heart of her. 'I'm not. I know you'll look after him better than anyone. You're an angel, Zoë. Some girls would be berating me for my colossal cheek after the way things have been—calling you at that hour of the night.'

'Ah—but I'm not "some girls".'

'No, you're not. You're a very special, very exceptional one. And I'm a lucky man to have you around.' There was a pause while Zoë savoured the glow caused by his words, then Ross got back to business again. 'I ought to have Helen's family's telephone number in case it's necessary to ring them urgently. Could you get it for me? There's an address book in my room, in the drawer of the bedside table. A black book at the right-hand side of the drawer, I think.'

'Hang on. I'll go and look.'

Zoë put down the phone and ran upstairs. The book was where Ross had said. In her haste she pulled out other papers with it, scattering them on the floor. She left them to be picked up later, and spoke to him from the extension on the bedside table.

'Hello? Are you there? I've got the book.'

'I'm here. The name is Frazer.'

She turned the pages. 'Here it is, I think. A Carlisle number?' She read it out to him.

'Thanks, Zoë. Just pray that I only have to call them to say all's well, won't you? And don't wait up. Pick your room and get some sleep if you can. You'll find the beds are all made up. I could be here hours yet.'

'All right, Ross,' she said. 'I'll be thinking about you. Goodnight.'

'Goodnight, love.' She thought he said 'love', but he

hung up so quickly that she doubted that she had heard
correctly. But the endearment, real or imaginary, started
off a drift of wishful thinking. She straightened the duvet
and plumped the pillows, then folded his black silk
pyjamas and stood foolishly hugging them while she
wondered what it would be like to be the sort of girl who
took a man at his ill-considered word and chose his own
bed to lie waiting for him in. The sort of girl who didn't
give a fig for a missing wife, the kind who knew what
she wanted and went all out to get it. But it was fruitless
thinking. She was not that kind of girl.

She went downstairs and put out lights, leaving only
the terrace light to welcome Ross home and the hall light
so that he would see her note telling him there was
something to eat in the kitchen.

It made sense to go to bed, she supposed, though she
couldn't imagine sleeping until she knew what had
happened. She chose the room opposite Jonathan's
where she could be sure of hearing him if he cried, a
chintzy, comfortable room.

It was only when she was undressed that she realised
that she had not thought to bring night clothes. If she
had to get up to Jonathan that could create problems.
And she would also want to go down when she heard
Ross come back. There seemed something distasteful in
the circumstances in going poking around among Helen's
clothes where there would no doubt be a nightdress.
Perhaps Ross wouldn't mind if she purloined a shirt and
dressing-gown from him.

She went back to his room and slid back a wardrobe
door. It was the wrong door, and she was confronted by
what could only be Alessandra's clothes. Bright, in a
multitude of fabrics, they moved slightly in the draught
the door had created. There was still a faint perfume
clinging to them. Zoë's throat constricted and she closed

the door with a slam, as though she had been confronted by a snake. Different images from her last thoughts in this room filled her mind—Ross burying his face in silks and velvets to breathe in the perfume and ease his longing for Alessandra. The sudden sight of the clothes made Ross's wife real, in the same way as Zoë's first glimpse of Jonathan had fleshed out what had until then only seemed the ghost of a marriage.

Oh—concentrate on what you're supposed to be doing. . .she told herself impatiently, and found the right door this time. There was a blue and white cotton check shirt that, with the sleeves well rolled up, made a voluminous and quite decent short nightdress. The man's short towelling robe behind the door was respectably long on her, and she took that too.

The phone rang as she was leaving the room, and Zoë ran back to answer it, sure that it would be Ross again.

'Hello?'

A man's voice answered. A strange voice, coming and going as the sound swelled and faded. 'I was hoping to speak to Mr Macallister. What number is that?' It sounded like a long-distance call.

'The right one. But Mr Macallister's not here.'

'Are you his housekeeper?'

The complications of explaining who she was and why she was there were too many. She decided that agreement was easier.

'Yes,' Zoë said firmly.

'Sorry to disturb you. I know it can't be a convenient time. Do you know when he'll be in?'

'I'm afraid not. Not for some time, I think.' It suddenly struck her that if she was speaking to a potential burglar she had told him all he wanted to know. 'Who are you, please?' she added.

'Tell him Hooper phoned. He'll know who I am.'

'Shall I give him a message? Or your number?'

'I shan't have a number, where I'm going. And I'm off right now, hence the highly inconvenient call.' The line crackled and whistled and eventually cleared again. 'Look,' the caller was saying, 'just say that I think I may have a lead at last.' Only then did Zoë realise to whom she was speaking. It was one of Ross's private investigators on the line. The enormity of what he had just said took the strength from her legs and she sank back on the bed. 'Just that, and no more,' the man was saying. '*May*. . .not definitely have. But tell him that if this comes good then there's every chance of a positive outcome to this job. He'll know what that means. And I'll be in touch as soon as I can. Got all that?'

'Yes,' Zoë said faintly. Was he saying that he thought it possible that he was going to find Aless alive?

'You'd better tell him, too, that I've got a chap taking me to somewhere called Tokemotu,' he spelled out the word, 'though it isn't on any map I've got.'

Zoë's hand holding the phone was shaking, she realised. 'I've made a note of that,' she told him.

'Good. If it comes to a search for me, you could have the one vital clue there, lady. So don't lose it.'

'I won't. Is there anything else you want me to say?'

'No. Sorry for the disturbance.'

The line buzzed, and Zoë put the phone down.

She cursed the ironic chance that had made her the one to take this call. It was cruel that she should have to watch Ross's joy as he seized on the first glimmer of hope there had been in the search for Alessandra. She wondered whether to take the easy way and write the message down. But somehow that risked making it seem more certain than it was. No. She must manage to give the message live and make sure Ross's hopes were not raised more than was justified by Hooper's phrasing and tone of voice.

The phone call put paid to any remote chance of sleep, and Zoë lay awake with Helen and Aless vying for space in her mind.

It was going up to four before she heard a vehicle approaching. She got out of bed and put on the robe, then went to the open stretch of landing where she could see down into the hall.

Ross let himself in and read her 'supper' note, then sensed her presence and looked up.

'Zoë—did I wake you? Or has Jonathan been playing up?'

'Neither. I haven't been asleep.' She came down the stairs. He looked very tired and the dark shadow of his beard matched the marks of fatigue under his eyes. 'How is Helen?' she asked him apprehensively.

'She going to be OK, thank goodness. They caught it just in time, apparently. The appendix was on the point of rupturing, so it was a close thing. They let me see her for a few seconds. She was more asleep than awake, but not in such pain any longer, thank the lord.'

Relief came before anything else, and Zoë put her hand on his arm spontaneously. 'I'm so *glad* you didn't have to use that number.'

'So am I,' Ross said with feeling, his face shedding some of its fatigue as he returned her smile. 'I'll phone Mr and Mrs Frazer at a more civilised hour and let them know what happened. Come into the kitchen with me while I tackle some of these refreshments you've laid on.'

He suddenly seemed to realise what she was wearing. The shirt and robe were so much too big for her that they had slipped off to expose one bare shoulder. Ross smiled again and gently hitched them up, making a shiver run down her spine at the touch of his hand. 'Look at you! That's a very fetching outfit, Miss Sutherland. It's a good job that this red-blooded male is well and truly physically and emotionally drained!'

Zoë busied herself pouring the coffee into two mugs and taking cling film off the sandwiches.

'I took your things—I hope you don't mind—because I felt superstitious about using something of Helen's. As though it might suggest to fate that she was going to have no further use for her clothes. Silly, really.'

Ross was still eyeing her approvingly, but at the same time making rapid inroads on the sandwiches. 'I'm going to feel differently about that shirt from now on.' He pushed the plate towards her. 'Aren't you going to have some of these? I find I'm quite hungry.'

'No, thanks.' She had been telling herself that there was no point in putting off what she had to do any longer. She took a deep breath and prepared to tell him about the phone call.

'Ross—someone rang up wanting to speak to you.'

'At this time of night? Who on earth was it?'

'A man called Hooper.'

His jaw froze and his eyes locked with hers. She had every shred of his attention. 'What did he say?'

'He thinks he may have a lead. He was very emphatic that I should say "may have".'

Just as she had known it would be, there was a sudden light in Ross's eyes. 'Something! At last! Tell me what he said. Did he leave a number?'

'I'm afraid not. He said he was about to move off somewhere—a place called Tokemotu. I've written it down as he spelled it out, but he warned that it didn't appear on the map he's got. He's going to be out of touch, he said. But he'll ring you again as soon as he can.'

'Damn!' Ross had leapt to his feet and he was pacing to and fro. 'Damn! Damn! Damn! Wouldn't you know that the first lead we've had—and yes, I know it's only a possibility—would come when I wasn't here to take the call?'

'I haven't told you quite everything, yet.' Zoë frowned, wanting to repeat the exact words, painful though they were to her. He said that if this lead came good, it could have a positive outcome. Yes—those were his exact words. He said you'd know what that meant.'

Ross's face blazed with uncontrollable joy, and Zoë could hardly bear to look at him.

'He means that there's a chance of Aless being found alive.' He stopped in front of her, and gripped her shoulders, forcing her to look at him. 'You realise that this is the very best thing that could happen? Oh, Zoë! How appropriate that you should be the one to give me such good news! If Hooper hadn't been pretty sure he'd never have phoned at this time of night. He'd have waited.'

He was so carried away by his feelings that he crushed her to him in the fiercest of hugs. Because it spilled over from his joy at the thought of his wife being found, his touch was unbearable to Zoë. She released herself as quickly as she could.

'I'm glad for you, Ross,' she managed to say. It felt like the biggest lie of her life.

'For us!' he emphasised, assuming again that she was as eager to find Aless as he was. He looked at her searchingly for a moment, and seemed to come back to earth. 'I think this waiting for developments is beginning to be as much of a trial for you as it is for me,' he said.

Were her feelings so obvious? Then she must make one last, superhuman effort. 'Hardly!' she said, with what she hoped was an understanding smile. 'But I'm sure you're dead beat now, Ross. Let's talk tomorrow, shall we? I'll get my things on and be off.'

'Off? Don't be silly,' he said with sudden energy. 'You're not going into the night again. Get some sleep here for what's left of it.'

'I doubt whether I shall sleep anywhere now. But I'd rather go. There's no point in hanging around here now you're back.'

His jaw set obstinately. 'I'd *like* you to stay.'

She gave a humourless little laugh. 'Now I know just how knackered you are. If you were in your right mind, you'd have been showing me the door long before now.' She reached for her car keys, which were on the kitchen table, but Ross snatched them up before she could get them.

'No,' he said firmly.

'Oh, for heaven's sake, Ross!' she said. 'Look at the time. I'm in no mood to play games. Give me those keys.'

'No,' he repeated. 'I've already had you driving through the dark once. That couldn't be avoided. This can. You can go home by daylight when it's far more suitable for a girl to be out and about.' He dropped the keys into his pocket, his eyes challenging her.

'I'm certainly not going to wrestle you for them,' Zoë told him sharply.

'Good. You're seeing sense.'

'I doubt that *you* are. One moment you're unwilling to have me in the house with no one around—and that's in broad daylight. The next you're being frightfully casual about my spending the night here.'

'Not casual. Caring.'

'Do you think Jean will see it that way when she turns up tomorrow? Or anyone else who finds out in the miraculous way they do up here?'

'Look, you silly girl,' he said, gripping her shoulders and giving her a little shake, 'tonight's been an emergency, hasn't it? I'm not creating another potential one by sending you out unnecessarily. Nor have I the least intention of turning out again myself to see you safely home. I don't give a damn what anybody thinks. Just for once you'll stay under my roof and either like it or lump it. Now get to bed. I was tired before you began all this. I'm exhausted at the end of it.'

He was obviously determined that she should stay. Zoë turned and stalked out of the kitchen.

'Zoë. . .?' His voice stopped her at the top of the stairs. She turned and looked down impatiently. 'You're a gem. And I'm deeply grateful for what you've done tonight.'

'Oh, well, that makes it all all right, I suppose,' she said ungraciously, and went off to shut herself in her room.

Jonathan cried just before dawn. Zoë had not slept a wink—her mind was too aroused by the night's happenings, and she went straight across to his room.

The little boy's head was turning restlessly from side to side but he didn't seem to be fully awake, so Zoë didn't lift him, just murmured reassuring nonsenses to him and stroked his silky, warm little head until he grew still. She sang all the nursery rhymes she could remember, very softly, letting the movement of her hand grow lighter and lighter. When his breathing had deepened into a regular slow rise and fall again, she backed out of the room and gently closed the door.

As she turned, she saw Ross coming towards her along the landing, shrugging on the top of his black pyjamas.

'Jonathan cried,' Zoë said, conscious of the fact that the blue and white shirt was sliding off her shoulder again. And that although it might be voluminous there suddenly seemed to be a considerable length of leg showing. 'I didn't think you would hear from your room.'

'I have an alarm connected,' he said. 'Helen and I take alternate nights to get up to him if necessary. In any case, I wasn't asleep.'

'I should have left him to you. Sorry,' she said stiffly, turning to go back into her room.

'Zoë. . .' His hand stopped her, holding her bare arm. 'I could have come, but I deliberately waited. I was listening to you. You sounded quite lovely.'

She wanted to curl up with embarrassment at the thought of there having been an audience for her songs and nonsense. 'I wasn't thinking I was giving a public performance. You should have come along and taken over.'

He released her arm, but slowly, his touch sliding lingeringly down over her wrist and fingertips. 'I didn't come, because it was so touching to hear how you were with Jonathan. I knew you didn't realise I was listening. That made it all the sweeter.'

'So I pass on the children's nurse score, do I?' she said with a flippancy she certainly did not feel. Melting inside from his touch, she wanted to fling herself into his arms, plead with him not to think of her as a nurse for his child, as a good friend for himself. She wanted to beg him to see her as a woman, and respond to her as a man with a man's love, not as an appreciative father and acquaintance.

But of course none of that was possible. She could imagine how he was reading her feelings, pitying her.

'You're meant to be so much more than a nurse, Zoë,' he was saying softly. 'Soon it will be different. You've been more understanding than I could ever have hoped these past weeks—but I know it's not always been easy. Just hang on to the fact that there's hope of an end in sight now—and then it will be *your* time.'

He made an almost imperceptible move towards her, and she shrank back. She wanted no consoling hug, no talk of 'the right man' being sure to turn up. No understanding pity from Ross.

He was still, aware of her recoiling from him. 'Yes, you're right, of course, my wise, wise Zoë,' he said, with the briefest of smiles. Then, after the lightest of touches on her hair, he turned and went back to his room.

Zoë closed her own door behind her and leaned against it.

Wise? If only he knew how far from wise she was. One moment he seemed to know the struggle she was undergoing with her feelings for him. The next he was calling her wise, when how on earth could he think her so? Her head and her heart ached with confusion and conflicting emotions.

She walked restlessly to and fro in her room. She had had such noble intentions in staying on here, but the closer Ross got to knowing that Aless could be alive the more she wanted to hold on to him instead of preparing herself for the moment when she must inevitably let him go.

She flung herself under the duvet eventually and tossed and turned until the window grew bright and she felt that if Ross hadn't left her car keys in the kitchen— and why had it not occurred to her earlier in this ghastly night that he might have done just that?—then she would walk down the Glen and over the hill and leave him with the problem of returning her car himself.

She was as quiet as a mouse getting dressed, and tiptoed down the stairs without making a single creak.

But she could have spared herself the caution. Ross was waiting in the kitchen doorway, fully dressed.

'I've made some tea. Come and have a cup,' he said.

'I'd rather have my car keys, thanks,' she told him shortly, holding out her hand and adding, because she hoped fervently that he too had not slept, 'And I hope you've had as good a night as I have.'

He took her keys from his pocket, but he didn't give them to her straight away. 'I'll give you the satisfaction of saying that last night was probably not a very good idea. I can't say I slept much before Jonathan awoke. And I certainly didn't sleep after that little encounter on the landing.' He looked extremely tired.

'You can't blame Jonathan for this morning's early rising. He's still fast asleep,' she said.

Ross looked at her oddly. 'I don't know that I blame Jonathan for the middle of the night either, but we'll gloss over that. Tom at the stables thinks me utterly crazy. I was over there while it was still grey light, taking a horse out, and I've been riding since then until a quarter of an hour ago. That should have worked some of the devil out of me.' He was staring at her, hands thrust in the pockets of his twill riding breeches, brooding. 'It was all a lie, you know.'

'What was?'

'Saying I didn't want you going back to the cottage in the dark. The truth is—I just wanted to keep you here.'

There was a silence while Zoë's tired mind failed to find any sense in what he had just said. 'Why?'

'What do you mean, why?'

'It's not complicated,' she said impatiently. 'Why did you want to keep me here?'

He breathed out noisily and ran his hands through his already tousled hair. 'Sometimes you have me completely baffled, Zoë. I think we understand each other perfectly, and then—wham! I'm up against a blank wall of incomprehension—like now.'

She shrugged. 'I'm just not up to this blind man's buff conversation at this hour of the day. Shall we accept mutual bafflement and go our separate ways?'

'No, we damned well shall not,' he said emphatically. 'I thought that you knew where I stood with regard to you. That it wasn't necessary to spell it out. But this peculiar attitude of yours last night, and then now. . . Zoë—haven't I made myself clear to you? Is that possible?'

She wanted to die at the thought of him bringing out into the open between them her feelings for him. It was her private grief—not his, to pick over and pity her for from the ivory tower of his love for Aless.

'You've made yourself perfectly clear. Both directly and indirectly,' she told him.

He looked suddenly drawn. 'Then—is it your own feelings that are the problem? Is that it? I made allowances for the fact that you were tired and worried about Helen last night—but even so I would have expected you to be a damned sight more pleased at the prospect of news of Aless. And I know you were not pleased at all, were you, Zoë?'

So that was why he had wanted her to stay on—so that she should have a chance this morning to whoop with joy for him? His preposterous suggestion brought all her pain and shame bubbling up to burst out of her.

'What do you expect from me?' she cried. 'Blood? I've stayed on Arran largely to give you moral support because you seemed to need it and I deluded myself that rightly or wrongly I owed it to you. I've been your social partner when you've chosen. I've taken an interest—*more* than an interest—in your child,' she stressed, her voice shaking with emotion, 'until you put a stop to that and told me to switch off the love for him that I could have felt. I've spent time at your house when you chose to invite me, and been kept away from it when you thought it prudent. I've even, now, been kept in it against my will. And on top of all that you have the gall to suggest that I haven't danced with enough joyful abandon because there may soon be news of your wife. Well, let me tell you this, Ross Macallister. Finding Aless is your business. Your joy. Not mine. Good friends go no further than I have done. My part in proceedings is over. You have no right to expect any stronger reaction from me. Is that clear enough for you?'

She was almost weeping with frustration, and he was staring at her, his face grey. 'What an uncomprehending fool I've been. . .' he said slowly.

'You and me, both!' she flung at him. Then, snatching her keys from him, she fled from the house, safe in the knowledge that Jonathan would keep him there. He wouldn't follow her.

Zoë didn't even remember that she had left the lights blazing in the cottage and the door wide open a lifetime ago. So she was unaware that someone had been in and checked for signs of crime before putting off the lights and jumping to the right, but at the same time the wrong conclusion about the reason for her sudden departure.

The phone rang as she was putting food down for Polly. Ross, Zoë thought dully, and didn't answer it. It rang and rang, making Polly put her ears back in disapproval and eventually stalk disgustedly out of the house.

Zoë was drained of all feeling. She would sleep now, and she wished that the sleep would turn into the one that lasted forever.

She went up to her room, closed the door, and once in

bed pulled the duvet over her head to cut out the dull, insistent sound of the phone.

So it was not surprising that a little later she didn't hear the knocking on the cottage door either.

CHAPTER EIGHT

IT WAS a tap on her bedroom door that penetrated Zoë's subconscious eventually. She blinked sleepily at her travelling clock. After eleven—so she'd slept a good four hours. She didn't feel much better for it. The tap came again, and this time she was fully aware of it.

'Who is it?' she called.

Fiona's cheerful face peered round the door. 'Sorry to do this, but I hammered on the door earlier to no avail, and Polly's raising the roof now at being shut out, so I thought I'd better check you were all right.'

Zoë yawned dismally, and felt very miserable indeed. She was far from all right. 'I'm fine. . .' she said unconvincingly, and surprised both herself and Fiona by producing a couple of fat tears to roll down her cheeks, with more threatening to follow.

'Hey! That doesn't look all right to me,' Fiona said. She hesitated. 'Look—I'll go and make some tea. Be back in a minute.'

While she was away, Zoë indulged in a weep the like of which she had not allowed herself for ages. When Fiona came back with a tray on which were tea and slices of hot buttered toast she was red-eyed but coming out of the storm.

'Sorry about that. I had no idea I was going to do it,' she said. 'Put it down to the kind of night I had.'

Fiona brought a chair over to the side of the bed and balanced the tray on it while she filled one teacup.

'I knew something was going on. There's yours. If you want me to join you in a cup, I will. If you'd rather

163

see me off, I'll go.' She dumped the plate of toast in Zoë's lap. 'But in any case eat that. Crying's exhausting.'

Zoë had an overwhelming feeling of the need to talk to someone. It was unusual for her, but she had confided in Fiona once already, and there was so much that she was bottling up inside herself at the moment.

'I'd like you to stay,' she said. 'I shall need help with this mountain of toast anyway.'

'Rubbish!' Fiona said robustly, but she helped herself to a piece as she perched at the foot of the bed and tackled it enthusiastically while Zoë made a token effort at nibbling hers.

'I went over to Innis Howe in the night,' she said by way of introduction.

'I guessed as much. I was the one who put off the lights and closed the cottage up, by the way, in case you wondered.'

'Lights?' Zoë said bemusedly.

'You left them blazing. And the door wide open.' She grinned. 'It must have been quite a persuasive summons!' The grin faded as quickly as it had appeared. 'Though the result of it doesn't look too good. What's Ross been up to?'

'If that grin meant that you were thinking what I think you were thinking, don't waste your time,' Zoë told her. 'Helen was taken violently ill—appendicitis, it turned out to be. Ross needed someone to stay with Jonathan while he got her over to the hospital.'

'Oh—that's tough. Poor Helen,' Fiona said. 'And she was only just back from her week off, wasn't she? Had she had trouble while she was away?'

'I don't know. It all happened so suddenly and so awfully that I don't think she had the chance to tell Ross anything about the week away.'

They talked a bit longer about the events of the night,

then Fiona looked questioningly at Zoë. 'So it's all left you feeling rather limp. No wonder.'

Zoë's eyes met hers. 'No, it wasn't just that.' She sighed. 'Fiona—I know I can rely on your not letting this go any further. I'm afraid I've made a bit of a fool of myself. That's the long and short of it.'

'Don't we all, one time or another?' Fiona looked shrewdly at Zoë. 'Am I right if I make a tentative guess that Ross Macallister gave you a bit of help with the process?'

'Yes. . .and no. It concerns him, but he doesn't know it. At least, I'd rather he didn't, but I suspect he does, if you understand what I mean.'

'The understanding has a fair way to go,' Fiona said. 'But it's Sunday. I've all the time in the world.'

Zoë gave up the pretence of eating toast and slumped against the pillows. 'It all goes back to when I was first here. I shut you up when you mentioned that time earlier on, didn't I? But you were right. There was something between Ross and me. Only I had stupid reasons for not going any further with it.'

'That's not exactly news to me,' Fiona said gently. 'I saw Ross after you'd left, don't forget. He didn't talk about it to anyone as far as I know, but he didn't have to. It showed on his face.'

'Not for too long, though,' Zoë said carefully, avoiding Fiona's eyes.

'Long enough to prove it mattered more than a little.'

Zoë picked at the duvet cover. 'Well, at least he got over it. He married, didn't he?'

'I have my own views on how that came about,' Fiona said.

'I *know* how it came about. He told me.'

Fiona looked sceptical. 'Maybe he did, but do we ever

really know the reasons we do things?' she said obscurely. 'And it didn't exactly last long, did it?'

'Only because an accident happened.'

'Before that! Come on, now, Zoë. See straight. It's hardly the sign of a successful marriage when one of the partners shoots off with someone else of the opposite sex for a lengthy jaunt, is it? And when the bolter leaves a child only a few weeks old whatever was wrong with the marriage looks a million times more serious.'

'Anyone can have a bad patch. And having a baby can make women feel very emotionally churned up. I know Ross understood that.'

'Well, we're theorising, aren't we? I'm sorry enough that the crazy woman met the fate she did. So let's not talk about her. What about you?'

Zoë met her eyes. 'I realised what I wanted far too late.'

Fiona's understanding smile shone out again. 'Once more you're not telling me anything new. We've all been sitting back complacently waiting for the happy ending. What's holding it up? You're here. Ross is free. People would have to be fools not to know there were hearts and blue-birds in the air. Why talk of being too late?'

'You don't understand. Ross has never stopped loving Alessandra. He's reopened the search for her.'

'Surely he doesn't think she's still alive? After all this time without a word?'

'There's every chance she might be. Last night I took a call from one of the private detectives he's employing. There's a strong possibility that she may be found alive.'

'Are you saying he'd take her back after all she's done? And after how she's been with Jonathan? I find that hard to believe. He'd have to be crazy.'

'I think he is, about Aless. He's so overjoyed at the thought of getting her back that it *kills* me. Now you know why I'm shattered after last night. Oh—I know I've no earthly right to feel like this. I should never have stayed on here. I thought I was equal to the situation, and I'm not.' She blew her nose dismally. 'And I know it's no use talking about it, and I really shouldn't in any case. But you caught me off guard. Sorry, Fiona. Just forget everything I said.'

Fiona looked thoughtfully at her, head on one side, considering. 'Are you sure you've got it right?' she said.

Zoë looked uncomprehendingly at her. 'What do you mean?'

'Well—let's go back to Ross falling in love with Aless. Have you seen a photograph of her?'

'No. There aren't any around at Innis Howe. I suppose it hurts too much.'

'I've got a picture I cut out of the *Arran Banner* at the time of the wedding. I think you should see it before I say any more. Will you look at it if I fetch it?'

'Know thine enemy'. . . The phrase came into Zoë's mind. She had half a desire to see this woman who could hold Ross's love against such odds. 'If you want me to. . .' she said slowly.

'Don't go away. I'll be back in a minute. I know exactly where it is.' Fiona galloped downstairs and in no time at all was back. She put the newspaper cutting in Zoë's hands, and Zoë could feel her watching for a reaction.

Oddly, there wasn't much of one. For some reason she didn't find the lovely face laughing up at Ross in the photograph at all surprising. Perhaps because she had thought so much about Aless, she felt that she had known exactly what she would look like.

'What do you think?' Fiona asked, looking intently at her.

'She's pretty much as Ross described her.'

'Doesn't she remind you of anyone?'

Zoë frowned. 'Maybe. . .but I can't think who. No. . . I don't think she does.'

'Try looking in the mirror,' Fiona said.

'You mean——?' Zoë looked at the photograph again. Aless was slender and long-limbed—a similar build to herself. She knew that she had blue eyes, because Ross had said as much. Her hair was long and glossy and dark—another point of similarity. Now that Fiona had pointed it out, the oval face and delicate, regular features were not unlike her own. Perhaps that was what had given her the sense of *déjà vu*. 'You compare that laughing face with mine?' she said.

'Mood. . .' Fiona said. 'Believe me, she was your type. I wasn't the only one to notice it. And I'm sure that's what made Ross think she was what he wanted. Is he a man to marry with the speed he did—ask yourself that? He really was devastated when you went away, Zoë. Then along came this stand-in—somebody he could fantasise about, maybe, though we'll never know that and I doubt whether he does. He thought she could replace you, if only subconsciously. But she wasn't you. It wasn't surprising that the whole house of cards came tumbling down.'

'You're wrong. I've seen how Ross feels. I know how eager he looks when he thinks he may be getting news of her, and how utterly cast down he is when there's nothing.'

'Has it never occurred to you that there could be an entirely different reason for this sudden reawakening of eagerness to settle the business of Aless? If a man had thoughts of marrying again, but knew that he couldn't before seven years were up—because that's how it is when a partner is believed but not proved dead, isn't it?—well, he would be eager to get at the truth, wouldn't he?'

Zoë stared at her, thunderstruck. 'What on earth, other than guesswork, makes you say that?'

'Several things. Not the least of which is the fact that Ross did his level best to ensure that you stayed around on Arran.'

'Well, there you're absolutely wrong. He offered me a job at the Trekking Centre and I turned it down. He made no attempt to persuade me.'

'Of course he didn't,' Fiona said impatiently. 'He wouldn't want to appear as obvious as that. And he'd already set up an alternative anchor in the form of the job at the school, hadn't he?'

'But I don't understand what you're saying. *You* told me about the secretary's job. It came via Alec, I thought.'

'Via Alec, because Ross had a word with him on the subject,' Fiona explained carefully and astonishingly. 'Believe me, Ross pushed you like mad for that job. He's chairman of the school's board of governors. I don't suppose he slipped you that bit of information.'

'No, he certainly didn't.' Zoë drew in a deep breath. 'I can't take all this in. You've got me totally confused.'

'I think you should at least mull it over.'

Zoë shook her head disbelievingly. 'But Ross has never said a word to make me think there could be any truth in what you're suggesting.'

'Well, he wouldn't, would he? He's such a damned honourable man. How could he say or suggest anything about the future when his own position was so uncertain?'

The phone rang suddenly, setting Zoë's heart racing.

'Oh!' she cried. 'That's sure to be him. I left on such a bad note this morning.'

Fiona stood up. 'Then you'd better answer it. And do think over what I've said. Don't jump to conclusions.'

She ran off downstairs and out of the cottage, while Zoë followed more slowly, pulling on her kimono. She took a couple of deep breaths before picking up the phone. 'Yes?'

'Deigning to answer your phone at last, are you?' Ross sounded tetchy—not in the least as though he were speaking to someone he cared about. Fiona was talking nonsense.

'Why? Have you tried before?' she said.

'You know damned well I have. Both shortly after you left Innis Howe and later on.'

'I've been asleep.' Zoë yawned to prove it. 'Only just surfaced, actually. I'm surprised you haven't been doing the same.'

'Don't wind me up any more than you already have done,' Ross said tersely. 'I don't take kindly to your habit of walking out on me when you know I can't follow you.'

She was gaining confidence. 'There was plenty of provocation. Don't forget that I didn't take kindly to being kept at Innis Howe against my inclination,' she retorted smartly.

He didn't answer for a moment, then he said in an altered tone, 'Zoë. . . I do *not* like parting from anyone on an unpleasant note.'

'Neither do I,' she conceded.

'So I'd like the chance to put things right. Come over to lunch.'

'I'm not even dressed yet. I've got to wash my hair. And I've a mountain of things to do.' Excuses were spilling out far too quickly.

'Is that your way of saying that you don't want to

come?' There was an edge to his voice again. He was obviously on a short fuse.

'I do have a life of my own to live,' she said.

She heard him sigh in her ear. 'Point taken. Well, that's that, then. I can't come to you. Jean's got lunch well on the way. What about tonight?'

Her mind was blank. 'Tonight?'

'The Friends of the Opera Gala Evening at the Dial house. I presume that's still on?'

The invitation to the big house in the north of the island had been made and accepted a fortnight ago. Too much had happened in the past twenty-four hours and she had quite forgotten it.

'I wasn't sure that we'd be able to go with Helen in hospital,' she said, covering up. 'Oh—have you phoned to see how she is?'

'Of course,' he said impatiently. 'She's making good progress. Don't create diversions. As far as I'm concerned, tonight's on. I got in touch with a friend in Glasgow who runs an agency this morning, and a temporary replacement for Helen will be coming over on the afternoon boat.'

'And you don't think it unwise to leave Jonathan with a stranger?'

'Are you trying to make complications?' he fired at her.

'No, I'm not.' She was genuinely offended. 'I was thinking about Jonathan.'

'Well—there's no need for any change of plan. The woman who's coming is a professional. She'll have had tea with Jonathan, and put him to bed with me around. By that time she won't be a stranger.'

'In that case, let's leave it that I'll see you this evening.'

'If that's the way it's got to be. I'll pick you up at eight. And Zoë. . .'

'Yes?'

His voice softened again. 'I've done nothing but think since you left. There's a lot to be said to put things right between us. But I'm not going to attempt to do that over the phone. Some time tonight, face to face, regardless of what else we do, we've got to have a real, clear, serious talk.'

'If you think it will achieve anything,' she said doubtfully, her voice little more than a whisper.

'It had better,' he answered grimly.

She didn't know what to think as she put the phone down. Was Ross simply implying that he wanted to make it clear to her that he had in no way meant to give her encouragement to feel as she did for him? Or could there possibly be a glimmer of truth in Fiona's astonishing theory? She went over what he had said again and again, but ended up as confused as ever. First she felt hope because of Ross's change of voice twice during the conversation. Then came despair as she recalled the edginess that had pervaded most of what he said.

She began to relive everything that had happened between the two of them since she came back to Arran, but it wasn't long before her mind was reeling with the effort of trying to balance what was said against what could have been meant.

'Oh—leave it!' she told herself. She was going to find out one way or the other tonight. And when all was said and done things couldn't reach a lower ebb than when she had left Innis Howe this morning, so what was there to fear?

She ordered herself to remember that she had lived and enjoyed life before Ross; she would live and enjoy life after him if she had to. She only wished she could believe a word she was saying to herself.

* * *

Things to do at the cottage occupied the middle of the day, then thoughts of the evening to come, which had been kept at bay by Zoë's hyperactive bustling around, began to predominate again.

She knew what she was going to wear that evening: a cream organdie dress with a finely pleated bodice and a soft floating skirt. She had bought it for the Scottish dancing occasions when she partnered Ross. She got it out, and the jewellery she intended wearing with it. Time crawled slowly on.

Towards the end of the afternoon Zoë drove into Brodick where she bought flowers and magazines, then took them over to the hospital for Helen, who was still too knocked out by the operation to have more than a brief chat.

'Ross was in early this afternoon,' she said wanly to Zoë. 'I'm surprised that he can bear to see me again after last night.'

'Do you remember much?' Zoë asked.

'It's all very blurred. In view of the bits I *can* remember, I think I'd rather forget the lot. Ross said he was picking up a temp from the mid-afternoon ferry for Jonathan. I hope she's all right. What a nuisance I am to everybody.' Weak tears threatened. 'And what a weeping wally!' She dashed them away impatiently.

'Don't be silly. You can't help this. Concentrate on getting better,' Zoë told her firmly.

A nurse brought a vase for the lilies and carnations. 'Tomorrow she'll be a different creature,' she said reassuringly. 'The first day's the worst. From then on it's uphill, rapidly. And that's official.'

Zoë stayed a few more moments, then left with the promise that she would be in again.

* * *

She was ready far too early that evening with almost an hour left to kick her heels before Ross was due to pick her up. Aware that she had done far too much hanging around and wondering, Zoë decided to take the path over the hill to Innis Howe. Better to walk than to wait. And, if she got there early, maybe they would get the talking over before the Gala Evening.

She rang Innis Howe to let Ross know what she was doing, and someone who introduced herself as the new nurse answered the phone.

'Mr Macallister's in the sitting-room talking to someone. He asked me to take calls,' she said in a young, friendly voice. 'I'll give him your message as soon as there's an opportunity.'

Zoë thanked her, then took off her pretty shoes and slipped on a pair of flatties that she could tackle the path in and picked up the bead-patterned white evening bag Ross had brought back from the mainland for her. He had given her this first present after she had taken a leather bag to a dance earlier on in the summer, 'spoiling the picture', as he told her.

Arran was looking particularly beautiful as she climbed. She stopped for a while at the top of the hill and sat looking out over their two worlds, her cottage and Ross's estate. The panorama of land and sea glowed in the evening sunlight, with the Sound a sheet of gold and only two boats in sight, one white-sailed, one blue. Zoë drank in the peace of it, and felt more calm in spirit than she had been all day.

As she began to walk downhill towards Innis Howe she saw that, most unusually, there was someone walking up the path towards her, quite a long way off. As they drew near to each other, Zoë realised that she was a stranger, which was even more odd because the path was almost a private link between Innistulach and Innis Howe.

The fair-haired girl called out when they were within speaking distance. 'Excuse me, but are you Zoë Sutherland?'

'That's right,' Zoë answered. 'Sorry—but do I know you?'

'We spoke a short while ago on the telephone. I'm from Innis Howe. I took your message.'

'Of course! That explains why the voice seemed to ring a bell if the face didn't. You're the new nurse for Jonathan?'

'I am. Ann Tremaine.' They shook hands and Ann explained, 'I was on my way to meet you, as a matter of fact. I tried to ring you back, but you must have already left. Mr Macallister came out of the lounge almost immediately after you'd called so I was able to give him your message, and he said I was to ring you back and ask you to wait at the cottage as he was going to be delayed because of his visitor. If you had already left and I was unable to speak to you I was to be sure and meet you on the path and ask you to go back and wait for him at home. Sorry about that.'

'No fault of yours,' Zoë said. 'I should have stuck to the original arrangement. Oh, well—I've enjoyed the walk so far. I'll enjoy it in reverse.'

The girl looked embarrassed, hesitated, and then said, 'Could I ask you something?'

'Fire away.'

'Do you know Mr Macallister well?'

'Fairly well.'

'I don't want you to think I'm prying into his affairs, but I was led to believe by the agency that he was a widower, but I'm rather wondering what sort of situation I've got myself into. You see, I was going towards the stairs with juice for Jonathan when this visitor arrived. Mr Macallister had opened the door, and I heard him say "My God! Alice!" Then this lady walked right in and stopped me, saying, "What have we here, Ross? You've not wasted much time," sort of jokily, And he said, "This is Jonathan's nurse. Ann, my wife."'

'He called her Aless. . .' Zoë said, feeling as though the breath had been crushed out of her. Yesterday there was the merest hint of Aless's existence. Today, she was here. No wonder Ross was so anxious to stop her from crashing in on the reunion. 'Aless is certainly his wife's name,' she said faintly. 'She—she's been away.'

'He seemed so surprised. . .'

'He would be. She was missing after an accident.'

'I *see*. Oh, well, that solves that little problem. I didn't like to think that there might be anything awkward in the situation. I hope you don't mind my asking you?' She seemed unaware that Zoë was suffering anything like the cataclysmic reaction going on in her at the moment.

'Of course not,' Zoë managed to say.

'Then I'll get back to my charge. He was fast asleep when I got back upstairs with the juice. A nice little boy. Goodbye!' With a bright wave, she was gone, running off down the path.

Zoë turned and began to walk blindly up the hill. Aless back. . . How could it be? Yesterday there had only been a possibility of finding her. How could she have walked into Innis Howe this evening? And yet she had. 'Ann, my wife', Ross had said. What kind of Aless had come back? Aless, the same, or Aless transformed?

She stopped, suddenly unable to bear the thought of Ross coming to tell her what had happened. All Fiona's fanciful theories lost substance and faded into insignificance in the light of tonight's momentous happening.

The very fact that Aless had come back to Arran was meaningful enough. And, if Ross had the chance of Jonathan's true mother back, what other future could he decide to elect than one based on reunion with the woman he had loved so much?

She would not wait at the cottage for him to come, glowing with sudden joy, to tell her why their planned evening together was off, and why it didn't matter a jot whether they ever talked again or not. She simply couldn't face him until she had managed to get her feelings under some sort of control. . .and wrapped some cloak of dignity around herself.

She cut down through the trees in the Glen to come out on the Innis Howe drive. She could hurry along to where it branched, and take the rough track up the Glen.

She felt like a wounded animal, desperate to be alone to lick her wounds. Desperate, too, to put as much distance as she could between herself and the man who all unknowingly, she was sure now, had inflicted them.

CHAPTER NINE

THE trekkers were winding back down the hillside opposite, but too far away to be an embarrassment. Zoë thrust her evening shoes and bag into a gap in the stones of the cairn that marked the beginning of the path up the Glen, not caring that both remained clearly visible. Let anyone who fancied them take them. What meaning had Ross's gift for her now? She was not going to want any reminder of him once she had left Arran, and leaving was the only sane course open to her now.

What a fool she had been to come back into Ross's orbit a second time. What a double fool ever to have got so closely involved in his life on the pretext of helping him. The first two lines of a poem by John Donne played themselves over and over in her mind, taunting her as she walked fiercely on:

> I am two fools, I know,
> For loving, and for saying so.

Well—at least she hadn't actually said so. She had been spared that humiliation. If she tried very hard, super-humanly hard, she might get out of this mess with Ross maybe suspecting, but only herself and Fiona truly any the wiser about her state of mind.

Fiona. . . Yes, that was where she had been really foolish. She regretted now that outpouring of feeling this morning. But it was done. No taking back what she had said. And Fiona would keep her counsel, she thought. She hoped.

Zoë walked on, seeing nothing but the pictures thrown

up in her mind by her emotions. At least she could
award full marks to Aless for merciful timing, she told
herself bitterly. Her turning up today had prevented the
heart-to-heart talk Ross was intent on having. Now she
could leave Arran for some trumped-up reason of her
own, and with dignity, not because Ross had brought
out into the open between them feelings that should
never have been given the chance to grow.

She walked on and on until she realised that the
ground was growing steeper and wilder and she was
needing to use hands as well as feet to climb the craggy
slopes of Ard Dun, the peak that crowned the end of
Glen Innis. Enough was enough. There was no point in
putting her safety at risk, and the sky was already
beginning to take on the indigo of twilight over in the
east away from the sunset. She sat down, suddenly aware
of the punishing speed with which she had raced up
from Innis Howe. She must turn back. She would be
neck and neck with the fading light as it was. The
initiative to get up and go was lacking, though. She told
herself that a couple of minutes to draw breath wouldn't
make much difference.

A luminous wash of red-gold was spreading across the
sky in the wake of the sunset. Already the evening star
was pinpointing its position, and in a gap in the rugged
peaks at the foot of the Glen a tiny flash of gold marked
a glimpse of the Sound. Never were there such sunsets
in any other part of the world—or, if there were, she
had never been aware of them. Oh. . .this beautiful, this
entrancing, this damnably lovely island. If only she had
never set foot on it again, clung to the illusion of hating
it, and never put herself once more in the orbit of the
man with whom it would always be irrevocably linked in
her memory.

She heard Ross's voice before she saw him, and it was

for a moment as though she had conjured him up from the depths of her mind.

'Zoë-ë-ë-ë-ë!'

Her name ricocheted from side to side of the Glen, sending a grouse clattering noisily up into the air from the heather further down. Zoë shrank back into a hollow of the rocky ledge where she had paused. The cry came again, and again the echoes rang with her name.

She could see him now, his tall figure dwarfed by the steep sides of the Glen that crowded in on the path. His jacket swung from one hand over his shoulder, and it was only the lightness of the shirt he was wearing that made him stand out against the rugged background. She remembered what Fiona had said about him: 'He's such a damned honourable man.' Even the return of the wife he had longed for had not made him forget the need to explain himself out of tonight. How on earth had he known where to come, though? She wished with all her heart that he had given her more time. But then, would all the time in the world be enough? She must do the best she could. She got slowly to her feet and made herself visible to him.

'Zoë!' He broke into a run, long legs leaping from stone to stone until he was within yards of her, looking up to where she stood, still as a statue, with only the slight movement of the skirt of her dress showing life. 'What on earth made you come all this way?' he asked.

'Absent-mindedness, I suppose. I was enjoying the evening. I just forgot the time and walked on.' That was quite good. Cool. She was playing it cool. . .explaining herself quite believably.

'Did you forget our plans for this evening, or turn against them?'

'I didn't forget. I assumed when I got your message via the new nurse that this evening was cancelled.'

He stared up at her. 'Did I send such a message? I think not. I merely asked Ann to tell you that I would be late.'

'Maybe. But when she explained the reason for your lateness, regarding tonight as off seemed the logical thing to do.'

Annoyance flickered across his face. 'She had no right to add to what I said!'

'Don't blame her. She's only a girl, and new. She had been told you were a widower. She found it a bit alarming to have a wife—and an accusing one—walking in on things.'

He frowned, thinking it over. 'I suppose you're right. I would have preferred to tell you myself, though.'

Zoë decided it was time to speed things up. There was no point in prolonging the agony. 'Ross—I can't believe that we're talking trivialities about such a momentous happening. Aren't you going to tell me how Aless turned up so suddenly?' Good. She had managed the right note of slightly scolding, friendly curiosity.

'I can scarcely believe it myself.' He moved as though to climb up to where she was standing.

'No! Don't come up here!' That was not so good. There had been panic in her voice. But she couldn't bear him to come any closer. 'There isn't room for two.'

'Then come down here.' He stretched a hand up towards her and she shrank involuntarily aside, stumbling on a loose stone. 'Zoë! For heaven's sake! You're going to break your neck,' he protested.

She sat down quickly, the soft fabric of her dress billowing out with the sudden movement. 'There. That's safe enough. Why don't you sit down too?'

He was studying her face. 'Are you still angry because of last night?'

'I still think it was a stupid business. But I don't

harbour grievances forever, Ross. I'm a little more mature than that.' She paused. 'How did you know I'd come up here, anyway?'

'Tom told me. He called in at the house with a query about tomorrow's trek, and caught me getting into the car. When I told him to get a move on because I was already late to pick you up, he said that he had seen someone setting off up the Glen in what looked like very unsuitable gear. He took a look through his binoculars and saw that it was you. That wasn't very mature, was it, Zoë? The light's beginning to go, and you know how quickly the weather can change.'

'With that red sunset? It's set fair, and you know it.'

'Why on earth did you leave your shoes and bag in the cairn? They weren't at all hidden. Anyone could have taken them.'

'Ross. . .' she said with heavy patience. 'Are you ever going to get round to telling me what happened about Aless?'

His face broke into a smile that stabbed her where it hurt. 'Sorry. I keep getting side-tracked, don't I? I suppose I'm not quite in my right mind yet.'

'I've been trying to work out how it could happen so quickly in the end. Your Mr Hooper can hardly have got to her—and yet she arrived here less than twenty-four hours after he phoned to say he could be on the trail.'

'That was pure coincidence. He's probably still rooting around, and I can't let him know until I hear from him again. Aless had been on her way back for some time, of course.' He pushed back his hair and looked up at Zoë with that incredulous smile again. 'I still can't believe it!'

'Is she all right?'

'She's fine. A bit thinner—which isn't surprising in view of what happened.'

'But not hurt at all?'

'No. Going back months to the time of the wreck, she and this Nick Adamson fellow were picked up by a local fisherman when the worst of the storm passed over. They'd lashed themselves to the keel of the capsized boat until then. They were taken back to one of the islands and looked after quite kindly, then Aless got this crazy idea of their becoming a pair of voluntary shipwrecked mariners with the intention of getting a book out of it. They had themselves taken to a fairly isolated island where there was fresh water, and a certain amount of edible fruits growing, and there they stayed for six months, surviving on what they could get from the sea and vegetation, with only a box of basic rations—the kind that might conceivably have been washed ashore with them had their circumstances been real, to be resorted to only in desperation.'

'They must be mad!' Zoë said with feeling. 'How can anyone come as close as they did to losing life, only to put it instantly at risk again? Six months of that!'

Ross smiled ruefully. 'I told you Aless had been pretty wild. I imagine this was the sort of caper her father hoped to get out of her system by anchoring her to me. With very little success. But they weren't quite as crazy as it sounds. They paid the chap who dropped them on the island to come back every three weeks and check up on them. Never took advantage of his visits in any way, though. And they swore him to secrecy.'

'But he must have spoken in the end—to Hooper, presumably?'

'Yes. Another typical bit of Aless behaviour, I think. They hitched a lift on a yacht that put in to the island, and when the poor chap came for his next three-weekly check-up I presume he found nothing and panicked. I shan't know until I hear from Hooper. None of that worries Aless, though. She's got her book, and plenty of publicity for it promised when it's published next spring. Plus a load of other madcap ideas they want to put into practice, I'm afraid.'

There was a little silence, then what he had said suddenly penetrated Zoë's mind. '*They* want to put into practice?' she said.

Ross look at her directly, expressionlessly. 'Oh, yes. She's enjoyed it all far too much not to want it to go on. Nick Adamson too, apparently.'

Zoë's fury against Aless for all she had made Ross go through took precedence for a moment over her own feelings.

'How *could* she?' she burst out. 'After all you've done to find her—to let you wait without knowing anything from the time they were picked up. She could have told you months ago what happened. Didn't she care in the least what you and her family were going through?'

'Evidently not.' He was watching her without emotion, hiding his hurt behind a mask of self-control.

'Oh, Ross!' She looked helplessly at him. It was bad enough having to cope with her own emotions, but to know what he must be suffering was easily as painful. 'You must be feeling. . .' Words failed her. What words could possibly express all he had gone through and was still going through?

'What *do* you think I am feeling?' he asked, as though needing to hear her put into words all the incoherent anger against Aless and empathy for him that she was stumbling over.

'I know you must be heartbroken for Jonathan,' she said, turning eyes that were far more eloquent than her words could ever be on him. 'Didn't she seem at all sorry that she had lost so many months of his life? Didn't she at least feel *that* when she saw him again?'

'She didn't see him. He was in bed when she arrived, and she "thought it better not to disturb him".'

Zoë's feelings got the better of her, and tears spilled over. Not for herself, not even for Ross. But for Ross's child.

'Oh, poor, poor Jonathan!' she choked. 'Hasn't she had any change of heart for him, then?'

'Maybe a little. She might have hidden behind a pretence of not wanting to upset him—though a stranger passing in the street would be as likely as she to do that—but she is at least thinking ahead with some vague idea of him as a probable part of her life now—though by no means a permanent one. She said that if, when he's old enough, he feels any interest in the kind of travelling that fascinates her, the she'll try to have him along.'

Ross's calm delivery of such cold sentiments made them all the worse.

'Why did she come back at all, if she's no different from when she went away?' Zoë said passionately.

'That's simple. She came back because Adamson persuaded her that if they were staying together it would be as well to "tidy things up", as she put it.'

'Staying together? Then she's no intention of coming back to you?'

He gave the briefest of smiles. 'What did you imagine would happen? That she was coming back to me, then making off with Nick Adamson whenever she felt like it, with my blessing? Surely not, Zoë. No. She and Adamson are staying in Brodick tonight, then tomorrow we meet at my solicitors to set the wheels in motion for divorce. Adamson struck me as being keen to take her on. I hope he knows what he's doing.'

Zoë looked at him, bemused. 'You mean he came to Innis Howe too?'

'Didn't Ann tell you that? No—come to think of it, she would have been upstairs with Jonathan when Aless said casually that Adamson was outside in the car, and I said that she might as well bring him in.'

She shook her head in slow disbelief. 'Ross, you are *incredible*. Most men would have gone out and beaten him up. Heaven knows—*I* would have. Do you have to be so *saintly* about it all?'

Ross sprang to his feet. 'Zoë, I'm coming up. This has gone on long enough. It's time we got down to some real talking.'

In seconds he was there, sitting down at her side, holding a folded handkerchief towards her. 'Dry your eyes. No more tears now.'

'Not even for Jonathan? You can be as tough and manly as you like, but what about him?' She used the handkerchief, and sat twisting it in her hands.

'Jonathan doesn't need your tears—though perhaps the fact that you are moved to weep for him is the thing that proves it most conclusively. At least—I hope that is so.' He put a hand over hers, resting in her lap. 'Zoë. . .you haven't been reading my mind at all, have you? I have been thinking all these weeks that we understood each other. . .an unspoken understanding, but one that was there. Can I possibly have been wrong? Was it pure chance that made you stay on here, and nothing more?'

She stared down at his hand, holding hers. 'I felt that I owed it to you. You told me it helped to have someone around who knew the whole story. And I couldn't help thinking that if I hadn't gone away in the first place none of your troubles would have happened.'

He lifted her hand and tapped it down in her lap impatiently. 'That's a reason from the past. What about the present? Was there nothing in the present that made you want to stay?'

'I had nothing else to do for the moment. . .' she said lamely.

'Let me make my own meaning clear at last, then,' he said. 'Maybe honest talk from me will bring out the same for you. Oh, Zoë! Do you really not know that from the moment you walked back into my life I've been consumed by the desire to keep you there? Why else do you think I worked so hard to put you off Clive? Why else do you imagine I reopened the search for Aless, if not to make the way clear for us?'

Zoë's heart was suddenly racing, her mouth dry with the shock of his words. The wonderful, incredible shock!

'I thought you were desperate to have Aless back,' she said shakily.

'I've proved myself capable of one mistake, but I would have to be a fool to make it twice over. Do you think me a fool?'

'Then—you're not heartbroken?' What a stupid word to apply to a rugged man like Ross, and yet she knew how close hearts could come to breaking.

'At the prospect of getting nearer to what I want more than anything?' His voice lowered and he added seriously, 'But do you want it too, Zoë? Or have I been deluding myself all this time?'

'O-o-oh!' All her pent-up feelings exploded in a cry that was a blend of anguish and pure joy. 'Why on *earth* didn't you *tell* me?'

Before she knew what was happening, Ross had leapt to his feet and swept her up into his arms, and he was scrambling down to the path. Her feet had barely touched the ground before she was crushed against him, having the breath and the tension and the sadness that had been there kissed out of her.

'If you only knew how much I have been wanting to do that!' Ross said breathlessly at last.

'Why on earth didn't you tell me?' she repeated, but gently this time, from the wonderful security of his arms.

'How could I? How could I ask you to hang around for six more years—because that was what it seemed it would have to be. There was every reason to think Aless was dead, but that's not good enough for the law. All I could do was keep you here by fair means or foul, and pray that some miracle—helped along as much as I was capable of doing—would cut short the agony.'

Zoë remembered Fiona's speculation about Ross's feelings—speculation which was turning out to be so accurate. Should she tell him? No, because that would bring a third person into a moment meant for just the two of them.

'I would have lived with you, if you had asked me,' she said simply.

'I didn't want that for you. I wanted you to be my wife, wear my ring.'

'Such careful behaviour. . .' she said, touching his cheek lovingly.

'Not always. Don't you remember when we were up at the loch? Look what happened when I didn't succeed in keeping myself on a tight rein.'

'And I thought it was just the kind of frustration any man could be expected to feel in the circumstances.'

'Not any man's frustration. It was pure, overwhelming Zoë frustration. And when I apologised you accused me of trying to behave like a bronze god.' He crushed her against him again, and kissed the hollow of her neck, her throat, her lips. 'Would you make the same accusation now?' he asked huskily.

Her arms tightened round his neck. 'I've got so many

years to make up for. And I'll do it, believe me. To you, and to Jonathan.'

The horses must have been moving towards them on the soft, peaty ground, not on the path, because the first Zoë and Ross knew of their presence was when Tom's voice called out,

'Just shows how wrong a man can be. I actually thought you might need help!'

He was riding Rex and leading Taffy. And he was close enough for them to see the broad grin on his face.

Ross was not in the least put out. He kept his arm firmly round Zoë as they turned to look at Tom.

'I need your help right now about as much as I need a black eye!' he said. 'Since you're here, though, Tom—and with as much tact as an elephant in a china shop, I might add—we'll have a ride home. It's going to be dark soon. So nice thought, man. But pretty poor timing.'

'Want me to take the lady?' Tom asked with false innocence.

'I get the lady,' Ross said, helping Zoë up into Taffy's saddle then leaping up behind her. 'If she can bear to wait just a little while longer,' he whispered softly in Zoë's ear.

She leaned her head back against his shoulder with a sigh of contentment.

'Waiting's easy,' she said, 'once you know that two of you are waiting together.'

While away the lazy days of late Summer with our new gift selection
Intimate Moments

Four Romances, new in paperback, from four favourite authors.
The perfect treat!

The Colour of the Sea
Rosemary Hammond

Had We Never Loved
Jeneth Murrey

The Heron Quest
Charlotte Lamb

Magic of the Baobab
Yvonne Whittal

Available from July 1991. Price: £6.40

Mills & Boon

Next month's Romances

Each month, you can choose from a world of variety in romance with Mills & Boon. These are the new titles to look out for next month.

DANGEROUS INTERLOPER Penny Jordan

BETRAYED Anne Mather

TEMPT ME NOT Susan Napier

FORBIDDEN ENCHANTMENT Patricia Wilson

STAY UNTIL DAWN Elizabeth Oldfield

LASTING LEGACY Kay Thorpe

FORBIDDEN PASSION Sarah Holland

OUTBACK MAN Miranda Lee

MAN OF TRUTH Jessica Marchant

CARIBBEAN DESIRE Cathy Williams

SHADOW IN THE WINGS Lee Stafford

RISK OF THE HEART Grace Green

THE PARIS TYPE Christine Greig

HEARTSONG Melinda Cross

THE OTHER WOMAN Jessica Steele

STARSIGN
FORTUNE IN THE STARS Kate Proctor

Available from Boots, Martins, John Menzies, W.H. Smith, Woolworths and other paperback stockists.

Also available from Mills and Boon Reader Service, P.O. Box 236, Thornton Road, Croydon, Surrey CR9 3RU.